THE SIXPENNY DEBT
AND OTHER
OXFORD STORIES

The frontispiece is taken from the cover image. Further images can be seen at www.valeriepetts.co.uk

The cover image is a copy of an Oxford watercolour by Valerie Petts, and is reproduced by kind permission of the artist.

Profits from this book will be shared with
The Oxford Night Shelter

THE SIXPENNY DEBT
AND OTHER
OXFORD STORIES

OxPens

CONTENTS

Tim Kirtley provided the sketch for *Tortoises of Turl Street*

EDUCATION IN ACTION

JANE GORDON-CUMMING

Dulcie was the scourge of the evening class. Which one? No, I don't mean any class in particular. Dulcie was the Scourge of the Evening Class, generic. And I use the term loosely, to include day-time classes, weekend courses, summer schools — Dulcie was the scourge of the lot.

You probably remember her, on that weird old bike, balancing her canvasses, or her yoga mat, or her half-upholstered chair, tottering up the Banbury Road to the Ferry Centre or down to Wellington Square. She'd wear fat, sweaty dresses in the summer, and bulging knitwear in the winter, which she'd remove, layer by layer, at intervals with a heave and a vast sigh.

I suppose she was lonely, and some kind soul had suggested she joined an evening class, in the way kind souls do, little thinking what they were inflicting on the rest of us. Dulcie can't really have belonged to everything — there are only so many hours in the week, after all — but she was certainly at all my classes, and everything my friends went to, and anything people one struck up a conversation with at a dinner-party happened to mention that they went to.

She was, as I said, the scourge of every class. She'd wriggle and rustle and drop things, and have to leave the room at least once to go the loo, and then be given a résumé of the ten minutes or so she had missed. If you had the misfortune to be sitting next to her, she would talk to you in a loud whisper just as the teacher was explaining something essential, and then demand in a slightly aggrieved way to have it repeated 'because Lorna and I didn't hear what you said'.

She was completely devoid either of natural talent, or the ability to assimilate what she was being taught, so she would spend most of the time looking at what her neighbours were doing. One learnt to dread the gust of honeysuckle perfume at one's shoulder, the breathy pause while Dulcie assessed your work, and the helpful little point of criticism she was inevitably moved to offer.

It was worse for the tutors. The new ones felt obliged to help her, spending half the class trying to instil what the rest of us had grasped in two minutes. The more experienced ones recognised a hardened attention-seeker and refused to give in. A few just couldn't take it, and several classes with Dulcie in them folded when their teachers decided that supply-teaching fourteen-year-olds in Blackbird Leys was a softer option.

We'd all been through the stage of feeling sorry for Dulcie. After all it's hard to believe anyone could be so irredeemably awful. One would give her a lift after class, accept a cup of coffee in her dreary flat in Wolvercote, hoping she might be better on her home ground, or perhaps reveal some enthralling secret from her past life which would explain her dreadfulness.

But Dulcie didn't improve upon acquaintance. Sitting in the half-caned chair drinking yeasty home-made wine and eating some lethal offering from 'Creative Cake-Making' while she showed off her muddy water-colours and tried to get you to write her essay on '19th Century Political Thinkers' for her was enough to subvert the most saintly good neighbour. Having finally made one's escape — and under two hours was considered a pretty good record — no one risked repeating the experience.

I've enlarged on Dulcie's character at some length, because you need to have no misapprehensions about how totally awful she was in order to appreciate the absolute necessity of what followed. It's all too easy to criticise when one doesn't have the full facts to hand.

It was during the coffee-break in 'Rite and Ritual in Ancient Burial Practices' that Meryl dropped the bombshell: 'Dulcie's going to join the Wine Appreciation Group!'

We looked at her in horror.

'How on earth did she find out about it?'

Dulcie was on the other side of the room, pestering poor Mr. Henning on the details of Roman winding-sheets.

'It's in the booklet. She goes through them every now and then in case she's missed anything.'

The Wine Appreciation Group was a bit of a scam really. It had started as an off-shoot from 'Fine Wines for the Uninitiated', and had degenerated, if you can call it that, into a cosy social evening. We let our hair down, did a little wine-tasting, pulled everyone else apart, and went home feeling pleased with the world. We paid a nominal sum, but it was highly subsidised by the Council so it had to be in the booklet. It was in tiny print, though, between a Play Scheme and a Theatre Group for the Disabled. We'd thought we were safe.

'She's signed up for next Thursday. What are we going to do?'

We watched gloomily as Mr. Henning demonstrated folding techniques with a table-cloth in the region of Dulcie's plump neck.

The same thought came to all of us. No one voiced it; there was no need.

Isn't it heart-warming how people pull together in any kind of emergency? No one wasted time discussing what to do, but only how to carry out what obviously had to be done. And I must here pay tribute to the benefits of extra-mural classes, because we simply couldn't have managed without the wide-ranging experience we had gained from Continuing Education.

'Motive, Means and Method in Contemporary Crime Fiction' had taught us the names of several almost undetectable poisons, and Shona is having an affair with a Chemistry don, so she can get whatever she wants from the lab. It was easy enough for Vivian to insert an appropriate amount into Dulcie's onion bhaji during 'A

Taste of India' — Mrs. Khan tends to go heavy on the chilli anyway. We chose something that would take an hour or so to work, and Vivian accepted the dreaded invitation to coffee after the class, and let the rest of us in to Dulcie's flat as soon as the thing had taken effect. We cleared the flat up a bit, left a note for the milkman, and set about a rumour that Dulcie had gone on an educational tour of the Greek Islands.

It was the 'Rite and Ritual' class Field Trip that weekend. We were going to visit the archaeological dig at Edbury Camp, which has good examples of ancient burials from several periods. We took careful notes, including which parts of the site were actually being excavated, and which areas looked as if they wouldn't be disturbed for some time, and late on Sunday evening we made a private visit of our own in Vanessa's people-carrier, with Dulcie strapped upright on one of the back seats.

We had chosen a more or less Anglo-Saxon rite for Dulcie. A cremation would have been easier to dispose of, but North Oxford is a Smokeless Zone, so that was out. We decided on a burial in the manner of a middle-class Saxon woman — the type who would have gone to evening classes if such things had been available then. By the time we'd finished, no one was subject to the slightest twinge of conscience that we hadn't done the right thing. We went to a great deal of trouble with every detail, and I don't think even Dulcie would have found anything to complain about.

Everyone contributed something. Sophie made a lovely urn at 'Intermediate Pottery' which we smashed into authentic-looking sherds, and Tanya burnt a corn dolly from 'Countryside Crafts' to provide environmental remains. We wrapped the body in some hand-woven fabric dyed with nettles and blackberry-juice from a course at Waterperry House for which I'd been trying to find a use for ages. Colin, the only man among us, produced a pair of old leather sandals, and Rosanna knocked out a quite creditable pair of disc-brooches from a tin of cling peaches at 'Creative Recycling — Don't Bin It, Mould It.'

We made Colin dig the grave — men have their uses — arranged the body carefully in a sub-foetal position, and covered it with a nice little tumulus, which might also have been taken for one of the spoil-heaps nearby. We performed a circle-dance round it we'd learned the previous week, poured a libation of Lebanese Chianti, and went home feeling the satisfaction of a job well done.

And ever since that day Continuing Education in Oxford has taken on a totally new lease of life. Enrolment figures have shot up in the past few years, as people begin to realise that classes are safe. Dulcie's disappearance has led to some speculation, of course, the most popular theory being that she has done a Shirley Valentine and settled down with a Greek waiter.

Every summer we take part in the Practical Archaeology Summer School at Edbury Camp, keeping a watching brief on the progress of the excavations. This year they moved the spoil-heaps and began to dig the area where we had buried Dulcie — our work was about to be put to the test!

We weren't unduly apprehensive. The grave had had plenty of time to mature, and should by now be indistinguishable from its Anglo-Saxon neighbours. It was quite exciting, really — like seeing your cake come out of the oven in 'Practical Baking'.

We watched the young volunteer who was excavating the critical spot, heard her cry of delight as she discovered what we knew to be there, and surged over with the rest of the site to see what we knew she had found.

More senior archaeologists were called over to uncover the rest of the body. It was exactly as we had hoped. The remains had decomposed in a most satisfactory way, with fragments of material, pottery and brooches lying just as they should be. The Site Director himself removed what was left of the leather sandals with tender care, and it was as he held them up to view that one of us clapped a guilty hand to a guilty mouth. I shan't say who, as it wouldn't be fair, but you can't trust a man to do anything, can you?

The Oxford Police are very thorough. Some idiot must have reported Dulcie missing, for they found her on a list, and it didn't take them long to make the connection with evening-classes and haul us in to St. Aldates for questioning.

Our efforts to talk our way out of it were positively Socratic — we'd all done 'Platonic Dialectic and 4th Century Greek Philosophers'. But despite Maggie's insistence that Dark Age trade routes were extremely wide-ranging, and Lavinia's quite incontrovertible argument that 'Of course the Anglo-Saxons spoke English — they invented it, didn't they?', it proved impossible to persuade the Inspector that a sandal found in an ancient grave might justifiably carry the inscription 'Made in Korea'.

CROSS PURPOSES

LORNA PEARSON

'Curiouser and curiouser!' thought Alice, and finding the phrase satisfactory turned round and said it, with her best smile — the one that made grown-ups smile back, as if by a spell. It was wasted, however, because Mr Dodgson was busy with his books again; and even her nurse — though it was never meant for *her* — had gone to sleep in the broken cane chair in the corner. But Mr Dodgson turned to her all the same, with a smile all ready.

'What have you found, my dear, that's even curiouser than all the other curiosities in this admittedly rather curious room?'

'This thing,' and she held up a sheet of square-ruled paper, 'with all the squiggles on it as well as the figures.'

'My dear, my dear, you mustn't look at *that*. It's a game for people who don't understand anything real.'

Alice was not listening, because she had thought of something that was worth a repetition of the best smile. 'Why is Mr Dodgson's head like a sheet of checked paper?'

'Dear me!' He pondered. 'I don't know at all. Curiouser and curiouser! You'll have to tell *me*.'

'I don't know,' said Alice. '*You* always know things like that.'

'Do I? How dreadful of me' (striking himself across the knuckles with the steel ruler).

'Why did you do that?'

'For forgetting it when I know it all the time really, *you* know. What was it again? "Why is Mr Dodgson's head like a sheet of squared paper?" It's really very easy, you know. "Because it follows its own rules to the end, in all directions."'

'You see!' said Alice.

'I haven't finished yet: "in all directions, even if — especially if — they run at cross purposes." ' He nodded.

'What are cross purposes?' Alice asked, sitting on the pile of books in the window.

'Cross purposes? Oh, dear, I was hoping you wouldn't ask me that.' He ran the dividers through his hair distractedly.

'What are they?'

'Well, let's see if we can make it out between us. You know what a *purpose* is?'

Alice had never met one with an indefinite article in front of it. 'You can do things *on* purpose,' she ventured.

'So you can: like doing them *on* Monday or *on* a table. Only you can't have a *cross* table — unless it's *cross-grained*, like this one; but that's the walnut. Walnuts are very bad-tempered trees. That's why the nuts are so dry, and wrinkle their faces at you.'

'*Is* it a table?' Alice asked, bewildered; certainly his had more on it than she had ever seen on a table before, even when the dining-room at home had all the plate and the épergne that was shaped like a boat and the place-cards out, for an evening party.

'It's like an *arithmetic* table sometimes. No: *I* remember. I forget sometimes,' he sighed.

'Hit yourself over the knuckles again, then,' said Alice enthusiastically, smiling without thinking.

Mr Dodgson puckered his lips and his forehead. '*Must* I?'

'You did the other time.'

'But I didn't know it was going to hurt then,' said Mr Dodgson, turning his toes in pathetically.

'Shall I do it?' Alice asked, getting up in answer to her own question. Mr Dodgson looked more uncomfortable than ever at having the decision thus taken out of his hands.

'You won't hit *very* hard, will you?' he said, squeezing

his voice out very small through very small squeezed lips, as if he were going to cry.

'Not *very*,' said Alice, after careful thought.

'Promise?'

'Promise.'

He handed her the ruler with such a shaking hand that the ruler shook with it, and it was difficult to take it. 'You're doing it on purpose!' she cried.

'I'm not, then — there!' He clenched both fists on the ruler to keep it still. Alice pulled it hard until it came out: it was warm at the end he had been holding, because he had been tapping it on his knee for a long time.

'*Promise?*'

'Promise!'

He held out the shaking hand, and she struck, harder than she would have done if the hand had not been moving about so. She looked up at him guiltily. He had crumpled up inside his clothes, as if he and his coat and inexpressibles (that was the grown-up word) had been hanging on a washing-line and all fallen off in a heap.

'You *promised*!' he whimpered, his toes turning in farther than ever.

Alice knew it was her fault, and felt so uncomfortable that she hardened her heart quickly. 'What a baby you are!' she cried.

'Ah, yes,' (Mr Dodgson sighed again, looking at his toes as if they had gone like that without his knowing), 'but then you see I was born one, so I can't help it.'

Alice had a feeling that there was something not quite right about this argument; but she could not decide what, so she said '*I* don't believe you know what a purpose is.'

He sat up. 'I'll show you one!'

'You haven't got one!' — for her heart was still hard against him: she could feel it in her throat, making her quite breathless.

'I have, then!' He jumped up from his chair. '*Shall* I show you?'

'Yes!' But the tone of her voice was still against him.

'Give me your hand and I will.' Her hand was as stiff

as if it had her heart in it. He wrapped it up in his, and led her in and out of the piles of books on the floor to the fire-place, where the cat rumbled with a gentle mechanism on the cold tiles. 'There!' he said, pointing with his free hand.

'Where?' Her hand was beginning to thaw accidentally.

'Why, there!'

'There's nothing there!' she cried with an urgency that a minute before she would have refused him with all her might.

'Yes, there is: look.'

'A fire-place!' She was becoming desperate.

'And what else?'

'Wood! A cat!'

'A *purrrrrrrr*-puss!'

There was a little, sounding silence, such as follows the drop of a teaspoon on a flagged floor; the cat rumbled as if, like the cat in the Norse fairy-tale, it supported the mechanism of the world, which went on turning round them.

'*Oh*!' she exclaimed at last, and wrenched her hand free to set it and its pair on her hips.

'Isn't it?' he asked.

She found difficulty in denying it. There was something the matter with the explanation, however, and she remembered what. 'You said a *cross* purr-puss.'

'But she *is* when you pull her tail.'

Alice looked at the cat, thinking. He sat on his heels and stroked it; she went down beside him, wobbling, and had an inspiration. 'When you pull her tail she *stops* purring.'

'And that's what makes her cross,' he explained, watching his hand smoothing itself along the warm fur. 'She *likes* purring, you know, and she doesn't like having to stop; it's like the way a kettle stops singing when you take it away from a nice warm stove — and looks blacker than ever, too — '

'Why does she stop, then, if she doesn't want to?'

He looked at her. 'I suppose there are lots of things

that have to stop if you pull a lever.'

She lost her balance and sat down hard on the rug, shaking with giggles. 'You are *silly*!' she said, panting.

He had touched the lever he wanted at last; he watched her with a small smile.

'Mrs Liddell to see you, sir,' said the college scout, from behind the closed door.

Mr Dodgson's face made a rapid movement, seeming to have passed through regret before settling in what looked like satisfaction: as if he would have said 'At just the right time: sooner or later and it would have been the wrong one.' He said aloud 'Dear me! I had almost forgotten her. Do please send her up.'

Alice was sitting on the cold fender when he turned round, and her face had closed to him again, as if it were a grown-up's that one sees in a drawing-room.

'Our mamma runs as regular as clockwork,' he said, after taking her in and reflecting.

'She's not *your* mamma.'

It was curious — it *was* curious — but he could think of nothing to say; nothing at all. He looked at her, at her small knees bonnetted in the flounce of her frock, at the half-moons of hair falling randomly inside and outside her collar, at her mouth shut secretively like a bud and her eyes open, also secretively, like high windows in an empty house. She looked at him and saw that he wore black, and had strange large hands, and some eyes, a nose and a mouth, like a face that you draw. Meanwhile Mrs Liddell's footsteps moved up the stairs towards them. The room filled suddenly with social voices; the nurse in her corner woke up, scrambled to her feet, and looked with beaming attention from one to another.

'Mrs Liddell: do, pray, come in. I'm afraid there is nowhere *at all* to sit down except where Alice is sitting, which is very down indeed: too down for us. But I forgot: my chair. Do sit on my chair: I assure you none of it is catching.'

'Thank you: I'm sure I wish it were. It must be agreeable to be so dreadfully clever, mustn't it, Alice?

But I do indeed see that your rooms are looking a little more — ah —'

'Scholastic: *do* say scholastic.'

'The very word: a little more scholastic and single-gentlemanlike than usual.'

'If *my* room looked like this,' said Alice, 'you would send me to bed without any tea.'

Mr Dodgson talked again promptly. 'I'm sure it would be a privilege and pleasure to be told by Mrs Liddell to go to bed without any tea: it would make me feel young again, and what greater privilege or pleasure is there, Mrs Liddell? But I suppose that's no consolation to Alice, unless, Alice, you were to try to pass the time, each time you're sent to bed without any tea, pretending it was the time before, when you *were* younger. I'm talking nonsense again: I *do* wish you would make me promise not to.'

'You wouldn't keep the promise,' said Alice, walking in hard-soled boots across the room towards her mother and turning back with a look of challenge.

'Now, Alice, that's a very wicked thing to say,' said two voices.

'It would be, Mrs Liddell, if it were a lie; but since it's all too true, alas, it's moral enough to have passed the lips of a bishop.'

'I told you so,' said Alice.

'You did indeed, my dear, you did indeed.' And then he was silent; the cat rumbled uninterrupted on the hearth.

'Purr-puss,' said Alice, with her utmost scorn, from among her mother's skirts. It recalled Mrs Liddell to hers — subconsciously, it may be.

'Well, Mr Dodgson, I must be taking Alice off your hands, as I'm sure you've had quite enough of *her* nonsense; and many thanks for being so patient and kind as always.'

'Not at all. Goodbye, Mrs Liddell.'

'Goodbye, Mr Dodgson.'

'*Such* an interesting house, or rather —' said the nurse.

'Not at all. Goodbye, Alice.'

'Say goodbye, Alice,' said the two voices.

Alice made a face that only Mr Dodgson was to see. 'Goodbye.'

Mr Dodgson shut the door on them and leaned a little towards it, listening to the footsteps on the stairs. When they had ceased he stood with downcast eyes by the door, suspended, as if he should have said something and could not; then he started up and set out resolutely towards his table. As he sat down and looked about, the steel ruler caught his eye. Hesitating, he put out his hand, which was not *quite* steady even yet, and touched it. It had grown cold again.

IF THE WIND IS RIGHT

ANGELA CECIL-REID

It was six o'clock on Sunday evening when Richard and Oscar arrived on Port Meadow. It was a soft golden evening at the end of a balmy June day. Picnickers had long gone, only dog walkers and lovers remained. The balloon was unpacked and lay spread out on the ground in front of Richard

'Oh God,' he muttered, staring at the billowing sea of rainbow coloured fabric. However had he let himself be persuaded into this ridiculous venture? What had seemed just possible when the blood in his veins had been well diluted by wine, now seemed to be an idea conceived in hell.

*****

The evening had started out well enough. No better, and no worse, than any other spent with the Bainforths during the six months since they had moved into Number 23, Kiln Close. Sally had knocked on the front door. A blue-painted affair, covered with tangling trails of creeper in the heart of Old Marston.

'How wonderful of you to come,' said Linda, as she ushered them inside, 'Oscar will be with us in just a moment. He's on the phone. But then he's always on the phone.' Waving a perfectly manicured hand in the direction of the garden she added, 'We're having dinner on the terrace. Do go and sit down, Richard. Oscar'll bring you a drink shortly.' She leant towards Sally, kissing her lightly on both cheeks, 'Shall I take your wrap? Then if you'll just give me a hand with the salad, we can catch up on the gossip.'

The women vanished and Richard made his way out onto the tiny patio. Oscar appeared from the kitchen holding a bottle of champagne. He was wearing a pale green polo shirt which showed off his golden tan. 'I thought we'd celebrate. After all you don't have a birthday every day, do you? He handed Richard a glass and filled it. There was a long silence, edgy and uncomfortable. But at last Oscar spoke. 'So how's life on the road then?'

Richard took a sip of champagne. The bubbles tingled on his tongue. How he longed for the smoothness of a beer. 'Not so bad. That new line in Norwegian frozen salmon fillets I was telling you about, that's going down a treat.'

'Oh . . . good,' said Oscar without enthusiasm. He leaned back in his chair and closed his eyes.

Richard took another sip. More of a gulp, this time. 'So, how's it been in your neck of the woods?'

Oscar opened his eyes, but he didn't look at Richard. He stared instead at the thatch of sweet smelling honeysuckle that covered the wall separating their two gardens. 'Good. Work's still keeping the wolf from the door.' He rolled a mouthful of champagne round his mouth. 'Ah yes,' he said appreciatively, 'Dom Perignon, nineteen ninety-six. A truly vintage year. Light, with a touch of apricot. Perfect. Don't you think so?'

'Oh, yes . . .' Richard hastily took another sip and rolled it as Oscar just had. The sour taste of it filled his mouth. He forced himself to smile. 'Top stuff.'

'And,' continued Oscar, 'there's talk of promotion to the Paris office.'

Richard glanced towards the open kitchen door through which he could see Linda clearly. She was talking animatedly to Sally, and as she talked her long, slender fingers moved smoothly through the silver waterfall of her hair. Richard wondered if her touch would be as cool as ice, or whether it would burn like the sun. Linda laughed. It was an attractive laugh; a laugh that was as warm as summer. Richard glanced at Oscar, 'You won't be moving away, will you?'

'Possibly.'

'That'd be a right shame.'

Oscar raised an eyebrow. 'Oh, I'm sure you'd soon fill any little gap that our departure might leave.' He picked up a remote control off the table and aimed it towards the kitchen.

The air immediately resounded with what Richard could only describe afterwards as a right royal screeching. As the noise throbbed through the garden he watched a flight of sparrows hightailing it out of the nearby maple tree, and heading east.

'La Bohème. You recognised it, of course?' asked Oscar as he turned his copper brown eyes on Richard.

'Of course,' agreed Richard, shifting uneasily in his chair.

Oscar hummed a few bars before musing, 'Don't you just love Puccini? His music is so full of passion and love. Mimi's death from consumption is surely one of the most beautiful yet tragic moments in opera. Don't you agree?'

'Oh, yes . . . Tragic,' said Richard, taking another gulp of his drink. He didn't half wish he could exchange these posh evenings that Sally was so flaming keen on, for an evening at the Victoria Arms with Pete and Lenny. At least he could be himself there. But, he reassured himself, Oscar couldn't possibly guess that his only experience of opera was limited to handing out programmes for a school production of 'The Pirates of Penzance.' And right painful that'd been.

'Now, Richard, I have something that I think you will like.' Oscar flashed a wide, white smile at him. 'Linda and I have been talking. This birthday, it's the great five zero, isn't it?'

Damn Sally, thought Richard as he adjusted his glasses, what had possessed the woman to go and let out his age? He tried to make light of it. 'I'm afraid so, but then don't they say life begins . . . ?'

'At forty.' Oscar completed the sentence with innocent satisfaction. 'Now, fifty is something special. We wanted to give you something unforgettable. A real treat. You remember telling us how much you enjoyed your trip in a glider when you were with your friends in the South of France. I know that was a long time ago. Too long. We thought it would be amusing for you to relive such a special event.'

Richard found himself staring at Oscar, as he tried to control his tumbling thoughts; what was he on about? Trip . . . gliding . . . South of France?

Then, with a ghastly lurch of his stomach, Richard remembered. It had been weeks ago, near the end of another long evening. A little exaggeration had seemed harmless at the time. The fact that he had once, as a teenager on a school trip, walked round a glider parked on Booker Airfield, near High Wycombe, had turned, under the influence of a touch too much wine, into a description of a flight he had never made over the Mediterranean coast. God, not only had he never flown in a glider, he'd never actually travelled further abroad than the Isle of Wight. Sweat prickled his skin, as he remembered how he had detailed the flight with some confidence, having recently watched a programme 'Gliding: Great Journeys Without Power.' He had been so convincing, even Sally had believed him, although she was all too aware that nowadays he got vertigo at the top of a six foot ladder. But he had placed the whole episode safely in his youth; long before Sally and he had met, and he might have been a very different person then. He looked at Oscar. He couldn't have booked him a session in a glider, could he? Richard felt sick.

'But this time we wanted to make it a bit different.' Oscar smiled his wide, white smile again. 'Something rather more gentle. After all none of us are as young as we were.'

Richard glanced sharply at Oscar. There was something in his tone that unsettled him.

Oscar went smoothly on. 'So I've booked a flight in a hot air balloon. Sally said you'd be thrilled.' He raised his glass in the direction of the kitchen. 'And I know you're free on Sunday evening.'

Richard realised he was staring at Oscar, as a rabbit might stare at a fox. He blinked and forced a smile. To say that the thought of flying in something that resembled a laundry basket high over Oxford did not appeal was an understatement. Oscar took a sip of champagne, but his eyes never left Richard's.

It was then that Richard realised that the only thing more awful than a trip in a hot air balloon was allowing Oscar to see his fear. 'Why, that's right generous of you. But of course I couldn't accept.'

Oscar raised an eyebrow, 'Why ever not? Linda and I insist. It's just a small thank you for the way you have entertained us since our arrival.'

A shiver of suspicion quivered at the edges of Richard's mind at Oscar's words: wasn't there something a touch odd about them? But Oscar smiled a warm and open smile and the thought was banished as if it had never been.

Richard said quickly, 'No problem. Honest. It's been great getting to know you too . . . both of you.'

Oscar gazed thoughtfully at him for a long moment. Then he gave a small laugh and then called out, 'Linda, do come out here. I've told Richard about our little present. He says he can't possibly accept. Do persuade him.'

Linda appeared at the open door. The light was behind her and Richard caught his breath at the halo of light that surrounded her, illuminating her hourglass figure. She came and stood beside him, and his nostrils were filled with the scent of honey and lavender.

'You must go up, dearest Richard. You really must. It would be such a disappointment if you didn't. We thought you'd be so thrilled.' Her mouth trembled with concern. She rested her hand lightly on his shoulder, and his skin burned under her touch.

He stared at her. Sweet Jesus, could this fantastic woman possibly fancy him? A short, middle-aged man with thinning hair and a waistline that just wasn't what it used to be. But she certainly seemed to be giving off the right signals. His mouth was like sandpaper, his skin blazed, the erratic drumming of his heart filled his ears. At last he managed to find his voice. 'Oh, well, then . . . it'd

be a right adventure . . . I'll go. Thanks . . . both of you.'
But he saw only Linda.

The rest of the evening passed in a haze. His fear
mixed with desire was a potent combination. He hardly
noticed Sally, as Linda continued to be attentive to him
throughout dinner. The one glance he did throw towards
his wife told him that she also appeared to be enjoying
herself; her elbows were on the table and she was looking
intently at Oscar. He was being so charming to her. It was
kind of him; for while Sally was attractive enough for her
age, she was considerably older than Oscar. And
compared to Linda she was, well, yes, he had to admit it,
she was a touch dumpy. While her dark hair was a nice
enough tone of chestnut, and her eyes were a reasonably
pretty hazel brown, her overall appearance really couldn't
compare with Linda's. He turned back to find Linda
gazing at him, her expression inscrutable. But even as he
was aware of the look, it vanished and her face flickered
into its familiar warmth.

'So it's agreed? If the wind's right you will go up with
Oscar on Sunday evening. He's a very good pilot.'

Richard took a moment to register her words.
'Oscar's the pilot?'

'Of course. It would not be nearly so much fun if
someone else took you, would it?' And she leant forward
and touched his hand with hers. The touch was as light as
a child's butterfly kiss.

Richard swallowed. 'Do you enjoy flying too?'

'Me?' she laughed softly, 'Oh, certainly not. I'm afraid
of heights. I think you're extraordinarily brave.'

'Not at all,' he shrugged, hoping he sounded casually
confident. 'But you mean it will be just Oscar and me?
You're not coming, even to watch us go up?'

'I'm afraid I have a meeting.' She looked deeply into
Richard's eyes. 'But I'll so look forward to hearing all
about it.'

*****

'Come on, Richard. Stop day-dreaming and give us a

hand. The sooner we get this balloon up in the air, the further we can go.'

Richard realised that Oscar was staring impatiently at him. 'Right,' he said, wiping his sweating palms on his shorts. He hardly dared imagine how far 'further' might be.

'This easterly breeze is perfect. Quite perfect,' said Oscar. 'We are supposed to avoid crossing over the city centre. This will take us out towards Witney. It's a very pleasant area to view from a balloon; all those attractive villages and the wonderful open countryside.'

Oscar went over to a van parked nearby and Richard could see him chatting to two men inside. He called over to Richard, 'They agree the conditions are good. Not too much wind and good thermals. So it's all stations go.'

There was a small trailer attached to the van and the two men got out of the cab and helped Oscar to pull off the tarpaulin cover. Then they began to unload a billowing mountain of rainbow-coloured material. 'Help us lay it out on the grass well away from the trees,' Oscar instructed Richard. 'Then if you hold the mouth open we'll start filling it with hot air.'

Richard did as he was instructed; the opening was as wide as he was tall. He waited for the gas burner to be lit; and as it roared into life it flamed blue then gold, and the noise of it filled his ears. Oscar directed the flame towards the mouth. Richard moved quickly to one side, concerned that he would be burnt, but the heat travelled harmlessly past him. He watched the heaving waves of feather light material gradually swelling. He was only half aware of Oscar and his assistants in the background busying themselves with ropes and anchors, and attaching the basket. At last the huge orb left the ground and hovered above Richard's head. He stared up it and felt as insignificant as an ant beside it.

Sally would have liked to see this, he thought, but she was visiting her mother. Margaret had rung after lunch and complained bitterly of neglect. Sally knew where her priorities lay.

'Ready?'

Oscar's voice startled Richard and before he could gather his thoughts, he found himself being guided toward the basket. It was far too small and flimsy. 'You're sure it's safe?'

'Of course. Just get in and hold on. That's all there is to it. Easy. Especially for an expert glider pilot.'

Richard threw a suspicious glance at Oscar, but he looked relaxed, friendly. And it would be bloody rude not to go, thought Richard as he climbed cautiously in. Oscar followed him, and the basket lurched wildly. Richard grasped the padded leather rim, holding on so tightly he could see his knuckles whitening.

'All right then?' Oscar leaned over the edge. 'Okay, Josh, release the ropes.' At the same time he opened the burner valve and the gas roared even more loudly than before. Richard couldn't help it; he turned away from Oscar and closed his eyes. But he couldn't escape the horrible churning in his stomach; they were on their way up.

'We'll carry on burning until we've gained enough height. More gentle than a glider, don't you think?'

Oh ... yes,' Richard managed, his eyes still shut, his back to Oscar.

'Beautiful, isn't it?'

'Great.'

'Right, I think we're high enough,' said Oscar after what seemed like forever. Suddenly everything went quiet.

Richard held his breath, waiting for the sensation of falling now that the gas had reduced from roaring to a gentle hissing. The relative silence was empty, terrible. He'd give anything, absolutely anything, to be on solid ground. Then, through his panic, he began to realise that the balloon was remaining steady. He took a deep shaking breath. He was still alive, for now. Gradually he became aware of Oscar's voice saying his name. He turned to see Oscar pulling a map from the bag at his feet. It was in a plastic wallet. 'Now if you take the map you can work out where we are.'

Richard shook his head, 'No . . . it's fine.' Map reading in a car was one thing. Thousands of feet up in the air it was quite another.

Oscar gave a small smile. 'But I really do need you to read the map. I have to know where the hazards are.'

Richard stared at Oscar. Why'd he said 'hazards'?

Oscar stared back unblinking. 'You know, power lines, radio masts and so on.'

Reluctantly Richard held out a hand for the map. 'Oh yes, of course. Right you are, then. I'll do my best.'

Cautiously he peered over the edge of the basket. Oxfordshire was spread out below him. Toy trees, model houses, patchwork fields cut through by roads like silver ribbons, decorated with tiny cars and lorries like moving beads; it was magic. Richard forgot his fear, and his vertigo, as he stared in wonder at the new world below. He spotted a strange, small shadow moving slowly across the ground. For a moment he wondered what it could be, then he realised it was the shadow of the balloon.

'So have you found where we are?' Oscar demanded.

'Not yet.' Richard hastily opened the map and studied it for a moment before peering back at the ground. Where was the Thames? Or the M40? Or Didcot Power Station for that matter? You could usually see that for bloody miles. It was so all flaming confusing. One road looked like another from up here.

'Come on. It's same as when you're in a glider. Just find a landmark.' There was an unfamiliar tone of exasperation in Oscar's voice.

'I'm trying, but it's been a long time.' Like forever, Richard added to himself as he desperately looked for something he recognised. He became aware that their shadow seemed to be crossing the ground more slowly.

'Breeze is dying down. If we go a bit higher we might pick up another air stream,' said Oscar. And the gas burner blazed. Richard could feel the balloon rise, but the shadow on the ground was stationary.

'Looks like we're suspended here for a while,' said Oscar. He smiled his wide, white smile. 'You know it's quite an interesting situation, isn't it?'

'Why?' Interesting was not the first word that had leapt into Richard's mind.

Oscar went on as if Richard hadn't spoken. 'It's lucky we're such good friends. After all you read of two people who dislike each other, getting trapped together. Things can really get out of hand. It can be dangerous.'

'Dangerous? Why?' Richard searched Oscar's face for clues. But Oscar wasn't looking at him: he was closing the burner right down.

The balloon hung silently in the slowly fading evening light as Oscar looked thoughtfully at Richard. His expression was unreadable. 'I mean, you hear of people who under such circumstances reveal a dreadful secret. For example,' he paused, his eyes fixed on Richard, 'that they are in love with the other's wife. That could lead to most unfortunate unpleasantness. It is vital after all to remain sensible and dignified under such circumstances. Don't you agree?'

'Oh . . . right.' Richard forced his face to remain expressionless, but his heart had begun to thump uncontrollably. So Oscar knew. What a fool he'd been. Had he really thought he could keep his feelings for Linda hidden? And what about her? Did Linda know? Richard felt his face blaze with uncontrollable heat. Oh God, God, bloody God. How could he ever face her again?

The basket jolted suddenly. Richard realised a breeze had got up. He shivered.

Oscar leant over the side. 'The wind's changed. We're heading back over the city. There's nothing we can do about it. We can't land here, too many houses. We need a decent sized field. I'll let the ground crew know.' He pulled a mobile from his pocket.

'Ground crew?' Richard heard his voice as if from a long way away. Oscar was being far too calm, far too casual. He could see the headlines: LOVE TRIANGLE MAN FALLS FROM BALLOON.

Oscar's voice interrupted his thoughts. 'The men in the van. They follow us. When we land they'll pick us up.

It's usually pretty easy nowadays with mobile phones, but now we're going back over the city; they'll really have their work cut out to keep up with us.' Oscar threw Richard another sphinx look. 'But of course you'd know all about that, wouldn't you? With all your gliding experience.'

Richard tried to keep his voice steady. 'As I said, it was a long time ago.'

Oscar was now talking on the mobile. Richard, grateful for the time to gather and control his thoughts, glanced down at the city spread out beneath him. The beauty of it momentarily took his full attention. There was Tom Tower, tall, pale and gleaming in the evening sun, and there the Radcliffe Camera, with its fat grey dome squatting in the heart of the university.

Then Oscar's words beat their way back into his brain. What was he going to say next? Should he admit his attraction for Linda? What if Oscar got violent? Richard shuddered; it was a bloody long way down. His fingers instinctively tightened on a nearby rope.

It was then he realised Oscar had finished his call and was talking to him again.

'. . . see, one can always tell these things. I know women. I'm never wrong. So, come on, Richard . . . what would you do if you knew someone you thought of as a friend, a really good friend, was in love with your wife . . . and that your wife was in love with him?'

Richard's heart began to dance wildly in his chest. This was bloody marvellous. Linda in love with him. In love with boring middle-aged Richard Green. His eyes closed. Linda was in his arms, soft, warm, smelling of honey and lavender. The blood sang through his body.

Then sanity returned and with a sickening thud he remembered that he was currently suspended thousands of feet above Oxford. With a very jealous husband. And he suddenly felt quite extraordinarily alone.

'Oh, I'm right sure no one would want to take your wife from you. Lovely as she is . . . of course.'

Then Richard stared in amazement as Oscar threw back his head and laughed, his teeth glowing red in the light of the sinking sun. Like blood.

'My wife? Oh, I know no one would want to take Linda.'

Richard thought he must have misheard. 'Pardon?'

'He'd only have to live with her for five minutes to find out she's completely useless at more or less everything. She looks good, of course. But that's hardly a reason for loving someone. No. Someone like me needs a woman with passion, warmth, a sense of humour. Living with Linda is about as rewarding as living with . . . a blow-up doll.'

It was as if someone had showered Richard with ice. His desire evaporated as suddenly as it had arrived, those few months ago. The Linda of his dreams didn't exist. That's how it would stay. And Oscar didn't know. Relief flooded through him.

Oscar continued, 'I'm sorry. I shouldn't be so harsh. After all if you did want to live with Linda it would be perfect.'

Richard stared at him. 'What would be perfect?'

'If you moved in with Linda. You know, you are taking this very well.'

'Taking what well?'

'Haven't you listened to a word I've been saying? I want Sally. I love her. And I believe she wants me.'

Richard had this strange sensation that he was drowning. 'You mean that you and Sally have been. . .' He couldn't finish. He had never before felt rage, pure incandescent rage. He wanted to wrap his fingers round Oscar's bronzed bloody neck and throttle the life out of him. He'd never flash that damned smile at him again.

'You must have had some idea.'

'I trusted you. I trusted Sally.'

'Don't blame her. She did nothing. It was me. I fell for her the first moment I saw her. Warm, clever, generous. Everything Linda isn't. At first I couldn't believe how little you valued her. But maybe familiarity spoilt the magic.'

That moment at dinner. Richard remembered how he had looked round and seen Sally with her elbows on the table and how she was gazing at Oscar. She used to look at him like that a long time ago. He should have guessed. He'd been so stupid. So blind. 'So Sally's said she wants to leave me? To live with you?'

'Didn't you listen? She doesn't have to say anything. I told you that I know how she feels.'

Richard realised that Oscar must have been telling him this when he was admiring the view of the city below. He glanced over the basket. The houses were closer now. Surely too close? 'Oscar,' he screamed, 'we're sinking!'

Oscar looked over the side. 'I'll give it a burn.' The gas roared. The balloon stopped its descent, but did not rise. Again Oscar peered out over the basket. For a long moment Richard stared at his bent back. Just one push, that'd be all it would take. But even as his hand moved towards Oscar, he realised that then he really would be alone. Alone in the balloon, with no idea of how to get down. His hand dropped.

Oscar suddenly called, 'Look, Richard. It's the most amazing thing. I think if the wind's right we'll be going right down our road. Yes. Can you see? There's your house. You can see it quite clearly.'

Richard looked. The balloon was only a hundred or so feet up. Suddenly he wanted to see Sally so much it hurt. How could he have been so stupid? He should never have taken her for granted. He'd beg her to stay. If she didn't, he'd kill Oscar — Oscar would never have her. Where was she? Richard peered down. Mr Larkin was in his garden; he looked up and waved. Oscar waved cheerfully back. Richard's hands clenched. How dare Oscar be so unconcerned, so casual; as if it were obvious that Sally would prefer him?

They were almost over his house now. No sign of Sally. Of course not, she was with Margaret. But wasn't that Sally's Focus parked in their driveway? She must have come back early. And now they were over Oscar's house. Linda suddenly appeared from a side door: she was carrying a tray into the garden. How could he ever have thought he loved her? All he wanted was Sally.

Then he saw her. She was sitting on the terrace in Oscar's garden. He realised with a horrible jolt, why she was there. Oh God, she was going to tell Linda that she was going away with Oscar. He felt sick. He could see that Oscar was also watching the women. There was something beside Sally's chair. He peered hard. Suitcases?

'No!' he shouted, hardly recognising the desperate sound of his voice,

The balloon drifted silently closer. Richard watched Linda reach the terrace and put down the tray. She sat beside Sally. Was this it? The moment when it would all end. Richard wanted to scream down, 'Don't say anything. You're not going. I love you, Sally. Stay. I'll change.'

But even as he opened his mouth, he saw Linda lean forward and take Sally in her arms. Warm copper and ice blond, entwined, inseparable.

For a moment it didn't make sense. Then he understood. The deceit, the passion, the plan to get him, and Oscar, out of the way. What fools the women had made of them both. He glanced at Oscar. His expression of goggle-eyed surprise was so ridiculous that Richard heard himself laughing aloud. Oscar wouldn't have Sally now.

But as suddenly as it had been born, the laugh died, for he realised that neither would he.

THE TORTOISES OF
TURL STREET

LINORA LAWRENCE

On the south side of Turl Street, towards the High Street end, lay a shop. Tall, narrow and somewhat dusty from the outside, it had small, old-fashioned windows and a narrow entrance. Once inside, however, it transformed itself into a magical world of jade, amber, shell, other semi-precious stones and materials all beautifully displayed, with not a speck of dust on them. The glass of the showcases gleamed, the velvet backcloth was always freshly brushed, the floor glowed with polished tiles. This fine emporium dealt in new and antique jewellery and accessories such as combs, mirrors, ornaments and boxes. You had never seen such glorious, wonderful boxes, all shapes, all sizes, so many different woods, some inlaid and some carved. Boxes made to contain precious objects but becoming precious in themselves. Some were writing cases, some were designed for the storage of tea, some for toiletries, some boxes small enough to contain only a single ring. Everything was of the highest quality, which was hardly surprising for the owner had exquisite taste and highly developed judgement which had come from years and years and years in the business. These days he never made a mistake when buying; indeed, he shouldn't after all the decades he had been trading and the experience he had garnered. Nor was there any reason why he shouldn't go on trading for many years to come, for they live to a great age, do tortoises.

'Mr T', as he was known in the trade, lived at Balliol

College and though devoted to his business made sure he found time every day, and at the weekends, to bask in the sunshine in the college gardens. If you are wondering how his business managed during the winter when most tortoises hibernate the answer is quite simple: the business carried on; he did not hibernate. The only reason tortoises hibernate is the cold and by keeping the shop very warm and using a sunlamp (supplied by the Bursar of Balliol) Hermann (that was his real name) felt no need to retire for all those months. He enjoyed his life, and obtained much satisfaction from his expertise in his field but sometimes he did think about the past.

If you are wondering why you have never seen him making his way to and from college on a regular basis, it is because he gave up crossing Broad Street some forty years ago when the road became excessively busy. And this brings us to the story of the tunnel. When the tunnel was first thought of Hermann had a companion, another tortoise, Nelson, who lived at Wadham College and who also ran a business in the Turl; indeed he still does, at the opposite end. They had been friends then and not rivals, not that there was any business rivalry between them for their businesses traded in totally different merchandise.

Nelson's business, at the Broad Street end of the Turl, was a delightful luggage shop. He sold top quality leather goods. His shop had three floors; the general popular goods were on the ground floor, medium-priced luggage, briefcases, handbags and so on, also umbrellas. The first floor, up a short flight of stairs, Nelson devoted, apart from his own back office, to the sale of top of the range exclusive leather goods. Kid gloves, exquisite handbags, purses and wallets good enough to eat, briefcases once bought that would last a lifetime and other luxury leather accessories. On the top floor he went to the other extreme and sold very cheap bargains and even secondhand items such as college trunks which the students needed all the time.

Nelson kept a beady eye, with the aid of mirrors, on anyone going upstairs to the top floor searching for a bargain. From his vantage point on the middle floor and with the aid of an old-fashioned speaking tube system he kept in touch with his assistant on the ground floor. All in all, he ran an extremely successful business which made money for his college, the owners of the premises.

The subject of tunnels had come up one Sunday in the 1960s when Nelson and Hermann were enjoying their elevenses of wild pansies (their colleges took care to grow tortoises' favourite foods for them). They fell to discussing the ever-increasing traffic.

'You take your life in your hands, crossing Broad Street,' declared Nelson.

'I couldn't agree more,' said Hermann, 'I had a very narrow escape on Friday evening.'

'We could do with our own private road,' said Nelson conversationally.

'Hmm,' mused Hermann. They munched on in companionable silence. 'No, not a road, a tunnel . . .'

'Yes!' exclaimed Nelson, startling Hermann considerably. 'Of course! Like the Bodleian tunnel! If the Bodleian Library can have a tunnel running under Broad Street then why shouldn't we have one too!'

Once Hermann got over the shock of Nelson's outburst he realised the potential of the suggestion. Tortoises have a tremendous capacity for digging and there is nothing they like better so, though it would clearly take time to dig a tunnel, it would be well worthwhile, and the tunnel wouldn't need to be very big, just enough for one tortoise to pass another at most.

Hermann worked it out. 'First of all you need to get from Wadham to Trinity,' he said. 'The first problem is crossing Parks Road .'

'Yes,' said Nelson. 'Once I get across Parks Road I cut across Trinity gardens and then we both have to get across Broad Street.'

'So, first we have to dig a tunnel between Wadham and Trinity. Then, dig a longer one under Broad Street.'

'Come to think of it, why dig one under Broad Street?' said Nelson boldly. 'Why not just dig a small connecting tunnel to link into the Bodleian tunnel and then hitch a ride on their book conveyor system?'

The idea was so bold that Hermann didn't know what to say at first, but the more he thought about it the more the idea appealed. It would mean a great deal less digging and while they loved digging that would take some time and the problem of the traffic was becoming more urgent every day.

'Don't you think someone might notice us using the tunnel?' he said.

'Oh, I think it would be best to be honest about it from the beginning,' said Nelson. 'I think we should go and ask permission from Bodley's Librarian!'

'We would save a lot of time if we used their transport system,' said Hermann. 'I think you're right: we should ask permission. Yes, we'll go and see Bodley's Librarian!'

And that is exactly what they did. The Librarian was a most reasonable person who saw their dilemma and, as members of Oxford colleges, felt they were entitled to some help. He said that to make things quite proper Nelson and Hermann should obtain Readers' tickets as they would be on library premises during their journeys. That wouldn't be a problem, they should go to the Admissions Office with proof that they were members of their respective colleges and tickets would be issued. Any time that the transport system wasn't running they would have to walk, of course, but it was still infinitely safer than crossing the road, especially for a tortoise!

So, with tickets safely obtained from the Admissions Officer, who hadn't even looked up from his desk but simply examined their paperwork, they started to plan the digging of the tunnels. The first tunnel would be the one running under Parks Road to link Wadham College gardens to Trinity College gardens for Nelson's benefit; the second, from a suitable point in the gardens coming up at a similarly suitable place at basement level in the New Library (as the part of the Bodleian on North side of

Broad Street is called). This tunnel would, of course, be used by both Nelson and Hermann and they planned it to come up near the head of the Conveyor. Being very fair-minded they agreed to share the digging equally and settled that they would dig the short tunnel first and then start work on the one under Parks Road.

And this was, in fact, what led to their forty-year quarrel. Tortoises, as was mentioned earlier, are very proud of their digging and word went round about what they were planning to do. It became a talking point, particularly among the lady tortoises. Now there was one extremely attractive tortoise called Caroline whom all the other male tortoises admired very much. So far, she hadn't shown any preference towards any one of the males in particular — things move slowly for tortoises. However, it soon became evident that she was very excited by all the talk of digging and without either Hermann or Nelson meaning it to happen talk of a competition began to circulate.

Digging the first short tunnel was a shared job with Hermann and Nelson taking turns digging and shifting soil — they decided to get on with it immediately so that they could take advantage of the long Easter weekend which was just coming up. This meant the Library would be shut for when they would actually emerge into the ground floor of the Bookstack. While they had permission in general for their scheme they instinctively felt it would be wise not to worry the staff with the details of what they were doing. This all went well and then it was time for the other tunnel — this was where the competition element entered in. They had decided, sensibly, that they should start digging from each side of Parks Road and aim to meet in the middle. They agreed on a starting date and met to take measurements.

Caroline confided to her best friend Grace that the idea of digging stimulated her far more than gazing at Hermann or Nelson, or any of the others sunbathing. It affected her more than watching them eat lots of dandelions or clover and far, far more than when they started their businesses, enterprising though that decidedly was. 'Hermann's business is so cold and hard,' she said to Grace. 'All those stones!'

'But he is such a respected authority,' said Grace. 'People come from London to consult him. Even from abroad, I've heard.'

'I know,' said Caroline. 'But that doesn't make me feel anything. Nor does Nelson's business, for that matter.'

'I think Hermann really likes you,' said Grace. 'I've seen him watching you.'

'So what?' said Caroline, tossing her head and pretending indifference. 'Why do you think so, anyway?'

'Oh, he tries to get near to you at feeding time or have you in his view when we're sunbathing and he's always bumping into you, as if by accident, but it happens too often to be an accident.'

'I hadn't noticed,' said Caroline archly. 'But anyway they'll be fully occupied with digging the tunnel from now on.' And this certainly proved to be true.

It was an ambitious project. On the day designated for starting (they had agreed to dig only at weekends and Mondays when their shops were shut) Hermann, with his supporters, stood at an agreed spot in Trinity College gardens and Nelson with his supporters stood at an equivalent spot in Wadham College gardens. They had agreed to start as the college clocks struck the hour and, supervised by their supporters, who acted as witnesses, they did.

Now, I mentioned earlier how much all tortoises love digging, they really do. So you can imagine that watching Hermann and Nelson at their respective ends of the tunnel digging away soon became very frustrating to the others. So much so that they began to drift away from their posts and started little digs of their own. It started with a few little scrapes; then just another few.

'I'll make just a tiny little hole for fun,' said Julian to himself.

'I'll dig just for a few minutes just to keep myself warm,' said Adrian.

'I'm going to keep in practice with a pretend tunnel,' said Gregory. And they were off.

Well, it wasn't too bad the first day, or even the second and third, they didn't get too carried away, they controlled themselves and stopped and came back and continued to supervise and measure what Hermann and Nelson had achieved. But every weekend there was less and less supervision and measuring, more and more unauthorised digging.

Finally, after many weeks, the day was reached when the two tunnels should meet and become one. The tortoises still met up at the beginning of the shift, had an energy-giving snack together and started the digging, ceremoniously enough, but they had long since started to turn a blind eye to each other's peripheral activities. This was what led to much bigger problems. The moment when the two tunnels should have become one, with a couple of last big scrapes from either side given by Hermann and Nelson's front legs, should have been witnessed by two other tortoises at either side. Well, for a start, no other tortoise remembered to go into the main tunnels for this event. And, secondly, the event didn't happen — a dreadful miscalculation had been made! Hermann and Nelson had got their measurements wrong. They had failed to dig in a straight line towards each other. Neither wanted to admit he had messed up the calculations, or failed to be on duty, so afterwards it was never clear which tortoise had gone wrong (perhaps both had) or how they resolved it, let alone who dug the most. The tunnel was finally linked but by means of a curious dog-leg affair, and, since Hermann and Nelson were too much gentlemen to make great claims for themselves, it was left to their supporters to tell the tale their own ways. To cut a long story short both teams declared their tortoise to be the champion digger. The news spread slowly, different little groups being told at different times. During the first evening Caroline was told Hermann was the winner and when Hermann himself appeared (Nelson was still in Wadham College gardens) Caroline felt quite overcome at the sight of her hero. She was so excited; she had never felt like this before; she could hardly wait for the others to stop making a fuss of Hermann. Finally she got him to herself. 'Oh, you must tell me all about it,' she said breathlessly. 'You must describe every detail, show me what you did with your front legs.'

'But I've told you everything already,' said Hermann and he turned and looked at Caroline who was silhouetted in the lights from the college windows. It was early evening and the moon was shining down on her and with that and the golden light from the windows she suddenly looked very beautiful and Hermann felt something click. And then he realized that for a long time now he had known that Caroline was beautiful and that he wanted her to be his very best friend, only it had just become clear to him. It was like suddenly knowing that he had always known. 'Actually, perhaps I should tell you more about it. I could demonstrate what I did with my legs. Why don't you come with me and I'll show you my end of the tunnel?' And that was it. No one saw Caroline or Hermann again for the rest of the night.

Everything would have been fine if only Hermann hadn't got involved with a very important customer at the shop just before closing time the next day. This made him late home and long before he got home Caroline had become caught up with Nelson and his group of supporters telling everyone that Nelson was the winner because no one would admit that the linking of the tunnels had not been witnessed and proper measurements had not been taken. Nelson and Hermann each honestly believed that he himself was, as his supporters had told him, the legitimate winner.

I don't think that Caroline positively disbelieved Hermann, I think she simply got carried away with the excitement of the moment, the magic seemed to happen all over again for her and it happened for Nelson too, for the first time, in his case. The team suggested a trip through the tunnel to Wadham College to celebrate and Caroline was swept along with some others. However, once at the other side she and Nelson, after a certain amount of partying, became separated from the crowd and Nelson started to demonstrate to her his digging techniques and Caroline forgot all about her promises to Hermann and lost herself to the image of the beautiful heroine welcoming home the conquering hero. Once again Caroline was not seen again until the following morning, only this time it was Nelson whom she was not seen with!

Hermann, of course, did not know exactly where Caroline was; he had the vague impression she had gone to a party and though he missed her he was not unduly worried. He even thought that she was being modest, not wanting to appear too eager. It did bother Hermann a bit that there was no sign of her the next morning at the normal grazing time when he would have expected to see her with Grace. But Grace was clearly on her own. Hermann had to go and open the shop so he didn't have time to ask where Caroline was. He hurried off expecting to meet Nelson and start using the new route together but there was no sign of Nelson. Feeling a bit put out Hermann nevertheless carried on and did the new journey by himself. It was an adventure but not as great an adventure as it would have been with a companion. He caught one of the first book trays as the conveyor started to roll for the day. He made sure he had his Reader's ticket in case he should be challenged, but he wasn't. The Library didn't have a lot of tortoise readers (in fact, they didn't have any) but they had so many readers who behaved like tortoises that no one spotted the difference. He emerged in the Old Schools' Quadrangle, passed through the South Gate with the Radcliffe Camera on his left and turned up Brasenose Lane, then left into his end of Turl Street. He arrived fresh and in good time to open his shop for 9.30 — his usual opening time. He spent a normal day in the shop and went home by tunnel feeling quite content. He arrived back at Balliol College in time for the evening graze and then he did begin to worry. There was still no Caroline. This time he did go up to

Grace and ask her if Caroline was ill, or was it something else? Grace clearly felt put on the spot: 'I don't know, I don't know,' she kept repeating.

'You don't know if she's ill or not?' demanded Hermann.

'I don't think she's ill; there's no reason why she should be ill.'

'But you don't know. Do you mean you haven't seen her for two days?'

'No, not since . . . since . . .' Her voice trailed away.

'Since when?'

'Since she went to Nelson's party on Tuesday evening!'

There! It was said and, although going to a party ordinarily wouldn't mean a thing, somehow Hermann knew, and Grace knew, that in this case it meant a great deal.

Nothing more was said. By the Friday Caroline had returned to Balliol for she had become bored in Wadham College gardens when Nelson had finally gone to his shop. And she missed Grace and her other confidantes.

No one knew how to handle the situation. To speak? Not to speak? To be casual? To demand an explanation? What was going to happen next? By now Nelson had heard from quite a few others that Caroline had spent the night with Hermann the night immediately before she was with him. Which one of them was she going to choose? Did either one of them want to be a candidate for being chosen? Think of the shame for the rejected one.

*****

In the end they all behaved in a tortoise-like manner and didn't do anything in a hurry. Caroline didn't choose either of them. She simply did nothing about it. After a few weeks, she confided to Grace that she now knew that, in the fullness of time, she was going to lay some eggs. 'But who is the father?' asked Grace. 'Are they Hermann's or Nelson's?'

Caroline didn't know. On the one hand, the first night

had been with Hermann, but on the other hand, she had spent three whole nights with Nelson because he had been willing to leave his shop shut for two whole days to keep her company. Caroline told some of her other girlfriends and word got around. Secretly Nelson and Hermann were both wondering which one of them was the father. Most of all Caroline wondered and then she did something that only tortoises can do which was to decide the eggs weren't going to be born for a very long time. The way tortoises are made means that in the wild if they know their eggs are going to be born at a time of, say, drought or famine, they can hold onto them and wait for a better time. They will have to be laid some day but they can wait for a very long time. And that is just what Caroline did. In fact she waited so long everyone forgot she was carrying any eggs at all.

Hermann and Nelson went on going to their shops every day and not speaking to each other. It had started out of embarrassment and it hardened into total habit. As a matter of fact, unknown to each, they still recommended each other's shops to customers but they never actually spoke. Without discussing it they timed their journeys so that they wouldn't meet. Hermann kept to his original opening times but Nelson opened later and closed later, finding, oddly enough, that he got more custom that way.

*****

And so it went on for years, and years, and years. Decades rolled into decades and it looked as if nothing would ever alter. Then, one day, something happened that changed everything.

It was all to do with the book conveyor in the Bodleian tunnel.

The system was developed especially for the library when it had to expand in the late 1930s. The original library on the south side of Broad Street was no longer big enough and it was decided to build a new, additional block on the opposite corner of Broad Street. That

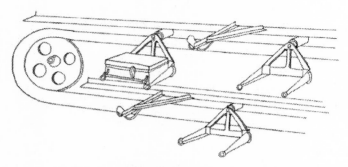

A Book Box on the Bodleian Book Conveyor System

building became known as the New Library and was connected to the Old Library by an underground tunnel with a book conveyor system running all day to take the books from the central core storage area in the New Library to the Reading Rooms in the Old Library. The whole thing became operational in 1945, and it worked very well but, like any machinery, it was not entirely unknown for it to break down. When it did it was always a big problem for the Library. It so happened that on the occasion when everything changed for the tortoises, after forty years, the book conveyor broke down on a Saturday morning just before the Library closed at 1.00 pm. The breakdown occurred so near closing time that it was decided simply to shut down the system and leave everything until Monday morning which was the earliest it could be repaired. This would have been fine except for the fact that Nelson had decided to hurry home slightly earlier than usual from the shop because the weather was so exceptionally beautiful (it was June) and he felt a great urge to sunbathe. As far as tortoises are concerned this is not just self-indulgence, it is a medical necessity for without sunbathing their shells would become unhealthy, so he obeyed his instinct and, leaving his two current assistants to lock up, he started off to go back to College at about 12.30 pm. Because he was going from South to North — the Old Library to the New — he had to travel on the upper line of trays on the conveyor (Nelson secretly found this more exciting than the morning journey on the lower level). He was sitting, as usual on the top of a book box, when the system suddenly juddered to a halt. So violent was the jerk that the book box (made of metal) was projected from the tray in front of him, its lid flying open at the same time releasing its contents. The book box struck Nelson, stunning him, on its way to the ground. The books hit his shell just as the tray came under a sensor trapping him as the conveyor came to rest. Nelson had been knocked out by Gibbons' *Decline and Fall of the Roman Empire*, Vol. II, and the fact that Gilbert White's *Natural History of Selbourne*, with all the nice bits about Timothy the tortoise, was on top of the Gibbon was no comfort at all. When he eventually came to a long time later he had no idea of the time. It always looked the same in the tunnel, dimly lit by safety lights in the ceiling and smelling of dry must.

After a while what must have happened dawned on him, although he didn't know why, and he didn't know under which weighty tome he was trapped. He squealed for help pathetically and then realised there was no point wasting his energy unless he heard footsteps coming up or down the tunnel; perhaps if he was lucky one of the Library engineers would need to use the tunnel — they worked through weekends and holidays maintaining the whole complex of buildings. The only trouble was that, if someone like that found him, the chances were that Bodley's Librarian would ban them from using the conveyor ever again, on the grounds of safety, and it did make such a difference to the speed of their journeys; plus there would be the embarrassment of Hermann knowing that it was through him that the ban had been imposed. Thinking of Hermann made him realise that his best hope was to try to attract his attention when he came home after shutting his shop at his normal time. The only fear was that Hermann might decide for once to take the overland route as it was such a beautiful day and coming home in the afternoons on a Saturday meant having to walk the whole distance anyway because the conveyor was always switched off.

Hermann shut much later than usual because he had had a special group of visitors from Holland who could only visit him on the Saturday afternoon. It was almost 5.00 pm when he shut the shop. He made sure his security grills were in place, he locked the door, gave a last admiring glance at his attractive window display (he never ceased to be proud of his shop) and set off. Up Turl Street, past the shoe shop that is as much a part of Oxford as the colleges; past the equally traditional gentlemen's outfitters, past the pen shop and the newsagents, and right into Brasenose Lane. The beggars had packed up for the day and only a lone student was playing Vivaldi on his violin on the corner attracting some coins from passing tourists. Hermann breathed in the beautiful air and the scent of the chestnuts bending down over the wall from Exeter College and fixed his eyes on the green grass round the Radcliffe Camera ahead of him. He did not seriously consider the possibility of going overland for a new hazard had presented itself of late — skateboarders! Yes, the latest craze manifested itself up and down Catte Street and along Broad Street, using the steps of the Clarendon Building as a run (on the same principle as a ski slope) and the speed at which these skateboarders travelled terrified Hermann. He had heard that a student had been knocked off her bike by one of them. No, however sweet the air and warm the afternoon sun, he was a creature of habit and caution and he determined to stick to his usual route and use the Bodleian tunnel. He squeezed sideways through the South Gate, a beautiful wrought iron construction padlocked at one o'clock on a Saturday afternoon but no barrier to a tortoise, and disappeared down his secret entrance in the north corner of the Quadrangle. He started his journey along the tunnel thinking of pansies and tender, young dandelion leaves for tea. Pitter patter went his firm little feet echoing along the tunnel and as he neared the far end to his amazement he recognized the sound of another tortoise's distress cry. A high-pitched anxious squeaking came from the deserted conveyor by the lift shaft. Hermann hurried on. Without thinking he shouted out, 'I'm here, don't worry, I'm coming.' He started to climb sideways up the thick wire barrier that enclosed the system.

'Thank goodness you've come.' Nelson was almost sobbing with relief. 'I'm trapped. The system stopped while I was still on it — I can't think why — it's never happened before.'

Hermann said, 'I think I saw an 'Out of Order' sign at the other end. It must have broken down just before closing time. Hang on, let me climb over to you.' There was a silence as Hermann climbed down to Tray No. 49. He could see what had happened and started to kick with his strong front legs at the offending volumes which had wedged themselves between Nelson's shell and the sensor on the conveyor system. If Tray 49 had stopped anywhere else the books might still have struck Nelson but they couldn't have trapped him. As it was, Nelson was completely stuck under the books which were under the arm of the sensor.

'Cor, they're heavy alright,' Hermann said as, with one last shove, he dislodged the books and they fell to the ground where they would be found on Monday morning. Poor Nelson, frightened, very thirsty, and with a nasty dent in his shell, trembled as Hermann helped him climb down very slowly to ground level. Hermann had to slow himself down and encourage Nelson who was shaking uncontrollably as they completed their journey. He also had to keep talking to him and reassuring him as he was clearly in shock and needed to be kept calm.

At last they found themselves in the fresh air of Trinity College gardens. 'I can't face another tunnel,' said Nelson desolately, thinking of the last leg of his journey back to Wadham.

'No, of course not. Come back with me to Balliol,' said Hermann. 'That's only crossing the garden and going through our hole in the wall. Then you can rest and have a nice refreshing drink and Grace or someone will see to your shell.'

He encouraged Nelson the last few yards of the journey, knowing as they went that it would be the lady tortoises who would fuss round and nurse Nelson, but, somehow, it didn't seem to matter any more. The crisis had taken over and broken the barrier of forty years of not speaking. The other tortoises stared like anything to see Hermann and Nelson emerge together through the hole in the wall. Then they realised Nelson was injured and they rallied round to help him. They made sure he got a good drink of water first, then the freshest, most tender leaves of his favourite plants and, most important of all for the healing of his shell, some ground eggshell which was put out for all of them by the Head Gardener to supplement their diet. Everyone brought their share to Nelson.

Nelson was too weak to keep repeating the story of what happened which left Hermann to relate it. But when he was too modest about his part in the rescue, Nelson did interrupt and say how brave and noble Hermann had been to be prepared to rescue him at all.

Caroline kept to the edge of the group and listened shyly. Much later on she told Grace she would really like to speak to Hermann but she didn't know how to begin.

'Come with me,' said Grace. After all these years she wasn't going to waste a minute. She marched Caroline over to where Hermann was feeding. 'Wait there,' she instructed Caroline, and walked firmly up to Hermann.

'Caroline would like to speak to you,' she said. 'But if you don't want to speak to her I shall go back to her and tell her so and that will be that — no need for embarrassment — it won't be mentioned again.'

'But, of course, she can speak to me if she would like to,' said Hermann. 'She always could have.'

Grace raised her eyebrows: well, she would have if she had had any. She did the tortoise equivalent and wrinkled her forehead. 'I don't think Caroline understood that,' she said. 'Anyway, never mind that now. If you'll speak to her I'll send her over.'

'Yes. Oh, yes!' said Herman. And that's how it happened. Grace gave Caroline a push and she came over and told Hermann how wonderful she thought he had been to overlook the past and rescue Nelson. 'I feel so ashamed,' she said.

'Well,' said Hermann, 'it was all such a long time ago — it's all like a dream now.'

'Yes,' agreed Caroline, 'except for the fact that I'm still . . . er, you know . . .' Her voice tailed off.

'Oh, yes, of course,' said Hermann, remembering. 'I suppose you're still carrying those eggs, aren't you? What do you want to do about them?'

'The truth is,' said Caroline, 'if I go ahead and lay them I don't know whose they'll be.'

'Does it really matter?' said Hermann. 'Why don't you just have them anyway and we'll all help look after them whoever they look like. If Nelson wants to join in and help that's fine, and if he doesn't for any reason, that's fine too.'

'Oh, you make such wonderful decisions,' breathed Caroline. 'Oh, thank you, thank you, I feel better already.'

After a bit more talk they agreed that Hermann should break the news to Nelson (Caroline felt too shy to do so) when Nelson was feeling better. Luckily Hermann decided to tell Nelson while he was still resting in Balliol gardens because, as soon as he returned to Wadham, having been escorted there by his friends, the Bursar saw his damaged tortoise shell and immediately arranged for him to be sent for rest and treatment to the Cotswold Wild Life Park where they had tortoises and turtles and knew how to treat them. While Nelson was there he fell in love with another tortoise, Rebecca, who was also recuperating after being injured. They became so attached to each other that, when eventually it was time for Nelson to return to Wadham, it was arranged that Rebecca, who had come from a broken home and had nowhere safe to go back to, would return with him and become a Wadham tortoise.

In the meantime, the required period of time had passed and, just as Nelson and Rebecca came back to Wadham, the little eggs that Caroline had laid were due to hatch. Caroline suspected what the result would be as three of the eggs had been one colour and the other three a slightly different colour. They hatched on a Sunday in September and, sure enough, there were three baby tortoises with one pattern of marking on their little shells and three with another pattern.

There were double celebrations. The Fellows of the College were so proud of the successful hatching of tortoise eggs, not a common event, that the babies were toasted at High Table. Hermann and Caroline were delighted with their new family. Then the news spread that Nelson had arrived home with a bride.

'I hope Nelson's prepared her for the situation.' said Hermann.

'Yes,' said Caroline, 'it might be a bit of a shock for her if he hasn't.'

The tortoises decided to throw yet another party to welcome Rebecca and to choose names for the babies — they felt they should all have a say in the matter.

Caroline and Rebecca met for the first time. 'What beautiful babies — you are clever to have hatched them all: you must be so proud of them,' said Rebecca.

Caroline glowed. 'Yes, they are handsome, aren't they? Just like their fathers. And what a pretty shell you have, my dear, such delicate markings.'

'Thank goodness for that,' said Nelson to Hermann. 'They seem to have hit it off.'

'Yes, 'said Hermann, 'potentially tricky situation but, as you say, it seems to be working out. We live in interesting times, Nelson, my dear fellow, interesting times!'

THE WINDOW

GINA CLAYE

I did not know where to go. I only knew I wanted to be outside. I leaned thankfully against the cold stone of the arched doorway and breathed in the scents of the summer night, the fresh earthy smell of the grass heightened by the shower of rain that had fallen earlier that evening. In the moonlight, standing as I was in Holywell Street, I could see the outline of New College roof with the spire beyond clearly etched against the night sky. There was no one about except for two students, holding hands, making their way through the Great Gate to the Front Quad. Their footsteps echoed on the cobbles, then died away. The night was silent again. I pressed my cheek against the cold stone and could almost believe I was part of the old buildings that surrounded me.

The darkness was suddenly broken by the light snapping on in a window very close to me at street level. It showed part of a college room converted into a kitchen. A woman, in jeans and a T-shirt, was standing facing the window, her hand on a tap, a pile of dishes on the nearby surface. Although her head was bent over her task, I could see she was young, about my age. She lifted plates and mugs in a calm unhurried manner. The process seemed endless. I watched her, mesmerized, lulled into reassurance as I watched an everyday task being done by another.

Suddenly she froze. A plate remained in mid-air for a split second and then was quickly put down. Wiping her hands on a towel, she turned her back and picked up a mobile on a wooden table near the door and put it to her ear. I could see she was slim, with long dark hair. As she listened her body grew tenser and tenser. She spoke only a couple of words and then thrust the mobile into the pocket of her jeans. She turned abruptly, seized a kettle, filled it with water, switched it on and then moved across to the door and out of my sight.

The window seemed very empty and I began to feel very much alone. The initiative was back with me now; I had to decide the next move. I was saved from this by the reappearance of the woman in the window. She had changed out of her jeans and was now wearing a pale blue dress. She switched the kettle back on, picked up two mugs, put a teabag in each, then poured boiling water into them. Suddenly she turned without warning and spoke. I could not see who she was speaking to but my gaze followed hers and as I looked, a man stepped into the picture. He was older than her and dressed in a casual but elegant way. They stood in profile, very close together, obviously intimate, yet he did not kiss her. I wondered why. He put his arms round her but she did not move towards him. He was still talking. She stayed silent with her eyes fixed on his face. They must have remained like this for some time. I wanted to hear what they were talking about. I almost felt I had a right to know.

As I watched I saw the man bend down and kiss her, then he was gone. He left that window frame as suddenly as he had entered it. The woman stood still for a long time, as motionless as I was, then slowly, mechanically, she took hold of one of the mugs. She emptied it carefully into the sink then picked up the dripping teabag. She squeezed it between her fingers and went on and on squeezing it until suddenly it split, over the sink, over the clean dishes, down the front of her pale blue dress. She held on to the taps as her head bent lower and lower and I could feel rather than see that she was crying.

I shivered violently in my thin clothes. I could no longer bear to watch the figure in the window. I was about to turn away, then my eyes were riveted once again by that square of light, when with an abrupt and violent movement the woman turned and rushed out of the kitchen. Where was she going? What was she going to do now? My head whirled. I couldn't think clearly. I clutched the stone doorway for support. In the overwhelming silence the bell in the tower of the University Church struck the half-hour, and then I became aware of another sound, the sound of ringing. I turned and ran into the kitchen. The mobile was still ringing insistently. I knew I had to answer it. I picked it up feverishly, but as I put it to my ear it stopped. I sank against the edge of the table and as I did so, dropped the mobile on the floor. As I bent to pick it up, I saw, for the first time, down the front of my pale blue dress, the dark ugly mark of tea stains.

CHERWELL ENCOUNTER

CHRIS BLOUNT

He is very tall and wears a calf-length herring-bone overcoat. He wears a trilby. He is pale with high cheekbones, dark hair sleeked back with no parting, perhaps just a hint of grey. He has a folded copy of *Le Figaro* under his arm. He is feeding the ducks.

Monique has not seen him before. She has come here every Sunday since Gilles . . . She doesn't know why she still comes. It is nearly a year. Why? *Pourquoi les doleurs?* It makes no sense. Does it increase the pain or expiate it? It has become a habit. The river is familiar. The ducks are the same. But ducks die like men and women. They are not the same ducks. Last year's ducklings, trailing their mother upstream towards the Botanical Gardens, are now fully grown. Some of them are now looking at her for bread, the others have succumbed to a fox, a heron, to hunger, cold or disease. *And so did Gilles. . . .*

Suddenly, startled by a car backfiring on Magdalen Bridge, the ducks fly off, leaving the apparent danger for the safety of Christchurch Meadow. Monique is also startled. She turns sharply and knocks *Le Figaro* to the ground.

'*Pardon,*' she says automatically, quickly retrieving the newspaper.

'*Française?*' he says quietly.

The bond of their common tongue breaks the ice and dissolves swiftly into trivia, about ducks, the English weather and why he carries *Le Figaro* under his arm. She is attracted to him. He is Philippe. He is strong. He is alone. No wife, girlfriend, children. Why? It is getting very cold. Almost unconsciously they talk their way gently along Deadman's Walk and through the gates between Merton and Corpus Christi. Neither has a plan as to where they are going. As they cross Oriel Square, he suggests a drink in The Bear. Monique readily agrees.

They are pleased to be in the warm. Monique sips her Pernod. Philippe struggles with a pint of Speckled Hen. He talks about his two little girls, whom his wife took back with her to Paris when they separated. He misses them very much. He hasn't seen them for a year, and then only for a few hours. Monique listens closely, talks about her job at the laboratory, but says nothing about Gilles.

Philippe does not ask. From time to time, he looks at her wedding finger. She has only just stopped wearing her ring. She took it off for the first time the other day, and has not put it back. She is not sure if this is significant. The ring has left its mark. Does Philippe notice this?

Philippe says he must go home to complete a draft for a lecture he is giving tomorrow. He is an international lawyer and has taken two years out to teach. It is now quite dark, and he asks if she would like to walk her home.

Monique accepts his offer and, as they walk, they talk about restaurants in Oxford. She complains how expensive the city is for eating out. They reach the door of her apartment block on Headington Hill.

Philippe kisses her lightly on each cheek, removing his hat, which is suddenly taken by a sharp gust of wind. He breaks off from the kiss to retrieve the hat. They laugh. He does not try to kiss her again but asks if she would like to have dinner with him during the week.

She finds herself saying she would prefer to cook him the Creole chicken he cannot find in Oxford. She has never previously invited a complete stranger to her home. He accepts and agrees to come to her flat in Granville Court on Wednesday.

Monday. Monique is at her home. She does not know Philippe's surname, his telephone number, nor his address. Strangely she is unconcerned.

Tuesday. Monique considers what to wear. She has always taken care to look chic. But since Gilles, she has noticed she has only bought clothes for work. She has had no social life. She is thirty-three, stands 1.74m and weighs 63kg. She still misses him so, but she is losing the fight to remember everything about him, his shoe size, his toothpaste, his favourite beer.

She has not been with a man since Gilles. At the beginning, she thought she never would. Monique has thrown herself into her work. She has been on research trips to New York, to Sao Paulo, to Shanghai. From time to time, she has been home to see her parents in Tours. She does not want to think about the future. Monique assumes she will always be at home.

Sometimes she wants a baby, but only with Gilles, and then she falls asleep crying.

She thinks about Philippe. It would be nice to have someone to go out with. She begins to think further, but quickly rebukes herself. She does not want to think beyond Wednesday.

Wednesday. She buys chicken, rice, lentil and haricots. Also some fresh mango from the Covered Market. She is looking for some papaya. She knows she can buy Fleurie from the off-licence Bottoms Up at The Plain.

Philippe is late, but he atones for this by bringing two bottles of Laurent Perrier. He assures her the second bottle is for her to keep. He tells her she looks *'trés jolie'*. She blushes.

Monique is wearing a midnight blue Karen Millen with a diagonal hemline. She has also bought a new bra, to achieve a hint of cleavage. The hemline leaves reveals her left thigh, almost shamelessly exposed. Is this the real Monique? She wears her expensive Clarins foundation and mascara for the first time since Gilles' accident.

Philippe is kind. He explores her life with Gilles, tenderly and sympathetically. He does not intrude into her private grief. Dinner is perfect. Monique is quietly proud of herself. They are well into the second Laurent Perrier. Half of the Fleurie has been drunk. Monique's head is on Philippe's chest.

Philippe does not go home. He shares Monique's bed. Their lovemaking is intense. Monique has no regrets.

She recalls, '*Après la passion, il y a toujours une petite vente sur le dos*'.

Thursday. '*Philippe est parti. Il est peut-être depart.*' Monique is in her lab. She is pre-occupied with the affairs of science.

Sunday. Most of the leaves on the trees by the Cherwell have now fallen. On the ground are mostly yellow chestnut leaves with black spots. The same is true of the sycamore and beech leaves. The trees still look healthy. Only the weeping ash still has leaves. These will not fall until December.

Monique is feeding the ducks. A car backfires and the ducks fly up. She turns and sees a man she has never seen before. He is tall and fair and wearing a greatcoat. Monique thinks he might be German.

THE SIXPENNY DEBT

JANE STEMP

With a sigh Barty shifted on the bench, picked up his newly trimmed pen and dipped it in the ink. At the other end of the library half-a-dozen gentleman scholars were playing football with something — probably a book — and outside the window the sun was shining, as it had been shining last autumn, when he and Giles came to Oxford. Giles came because it was the thing you did if you were a gentleman, and Barty came to be Giles's servitor. If only he could get learning somewhere, somehow, then he could leave home for good. Barty could not like his step-mother, though she tried hard to be kind: besides, there were five other mouths to feed.

And then Giles had died of a fever. Barty had written, as he ought, to Giles's parents to tell them what had happened: but he could not bear to go back home. He'd lived so carefully that five whole shillings of his caution money were still left to pay his fees, and the college seemed to have assumed that he was paying somebody else for a corner to sleep in. Barty had managed to stay and learn, living on scraps and pennies earned from odd jobs; but there was the vacation ahead, and what then? Life was hard when you were only thirteen, and the spring sunshine seemed to mock all your hopes.

The scholars in the scrimmage at the far end of the library broke apart and hurtled towards him, shouting and laughing. Something small flew over Barty's head and slapped into the wall. It was a book, vellum-bound rather than cased in wood and leather, and so less damaged than might be expected. Barty picked it up and laid it flat.

'Who's that?' someone said.

'Oh, only Barty.' That was Rhys Thomas. 'Times are I think he sleeps here. Give us the book, Bar.'

'Go find another one,' Barty said peaceably.

'Take it off him, shall we?' the first boy said.

'No, leave him be. Baa-lamb's no trouble.'

Barty smiled to himself as they rollicked away again. He did sleep in the library most times. It should have been locked up, ever since the Principal was expelled by the Parliament men, but for all that it was usually open. The worst thing was, that it was directly over the buttery and kitchens, and the smell of cooking food sometimes drove him almost mad with hunger.

The sunshine flickered between the leaves and through the window, and danced on the pages of Aristotle in front of him. Absently Barty picked up the football book and slipped it into the sleeve of his gown. He would put it back when he went out.

After a while Barty lifted his head and listened: someone was playing a fiddle in the street outside, just too far away for the tune to be heard. The library was noisier than ever, and the faint music held enchantment.

Quietly he laid down his pen and walked to the window, where the casement had been torn out during the last St David's Day fight (Parliament said there were no saints, but the fight had happened all the same). Barty hitched up his gown, climbed out of the library, hung by his fingertips for a moment or two, and dropped into the street below.

Spring in the streets of Oxford was not the alluring thing it had seemed from within doors. There was dung all over the paving, and a deal of shouting in the market; but the fiddler was still there. Barty picked himself up and shook the worst of the mess from his gown; there was going to be trouble if he was reported out without a fellow-student, so he rolled it into a bundle and tucked it under one arm. For a while he leaned against the wall and listened to the fiddler, then followed him down the lane that led to Michael's Church, and so to Corn Market street. This brought them out by Bocardo above the North Gate, and Barty turned his back on it, as he always did, because he would rather not think what the prison must be like inside: but then someone called his name.

'Barty! Hoy, Bar!' So Barty turned again, squinted up against the bright sky, and said, 'Who's there?'

'It's me — Harry Thorpe from Lincoln. Barty, can you spare sixpence?'

'*Spare* it? I haven't got it.'

'Oh come, don't pinch pennies. You must have something. Or touch Giles for it — go on, Baa-lamb.'

'*Giles*?' Barty stared up where he could just see Harry's face at the barred window. 'Giles is *dead*, didn't you know?' And he ran away down the Corn Market, his feet slipping on loose grain, past the Carfax conduit and beyond it to the unfinished front of Christ Church.

An hour sitting under the willows at the riverside, and Barty still didn't know what to do next. He was beginning to feel hungrier than usual, but what bothered him more was Harry's face behind the bars. Giles would never have grudged Harry sixpence; and he, Barty, would have moved heaven and earth to buy Giles free. And so . . . but where *could* he find sixpence? Wearily Barty got to his feet, picked up his gown and shook it out. Something fell into the grass. He bent down, and picked up the book he hadn't meant to take out of the library.

You could be *hanged* for stealing. Barty's fingers tingled with cold shock. And then, as if it had been an egg waiting to hatch, the thought came into his head: that's at least sixpence. He looked at the book more closely. Over a hundred years old, and no notes at all in the margins; probably nobody had ever read it. Perhaps nobody would miss it. Barty swallowed, rolled up his gown again, and set off across the meadows. There was a bookseller's shop he knew of in the High Street, he had sometimes done odd jobs of writing for the owner. . . .

But when he reached Rafe Aubrey's window, only his daughter Constance was there. Barty took hold of his courage with both hands, ignored his conscience and said, 'I want to sell this book.' He held it out, and Constance Aubrey took it.

'Father isn't here,' she said. 'Will you come back tomorrow?'

'Tomorrow?' Barty said, dismayed.

Constance laughed. 'Is it the end of the world?'

'I do need sixpence.'

She looked at the book again. 'Surely it's worth that much. I'll give you sixpence, and you can come again for the rest.'

'Then perhaps,' Barty said, stammering a little as he thought of something else, 'eightpence?'

'It must be the end of the world,' Constance said, nodding, with a dimple in each cheek.

Barty hung his head: but he looked at Constance again. She was a few years older than he was, well dressed, evidently well looked after. He hoped she wouldn't be shocked. 'The sixpence is to pay a . . . a friend out of Bocardo. But if I had tuppence I could buy something to eat.'

Constance said, 'I see', and went away into the back of the shop. She was gone for a long time; it even seemed to be getting dark, and Barty, looking up, saw that the sky was black with cloud. Constance came back, one hand closed, and the other holding a satchel. 'Here.' She tipped a silver groat and two copper pennies into his hand. 'Sixpence. And here's food for you.'

'But —' Barty said, the bag dangling from his hand.

'You can keep the satchel. Father found it in the street, but the leather won't suit for binding.' Constance looked at Barty as he stood there unmoving. 'Is there something more?'

'Please,' he said, 'I need to buy the book back — some time. Will you . . . take care not to sell it?'

She said, 'I hear Father calling you Lambert, when you work here. Is your name Lambert?'

'Bartholomew Lambert, mistress,' Barty said, ducking his head in the nearest he could manage to a bow.

'Well, Bartholomew Lambert, I promise not to sell your book.'

Barty ducked his head again. 'Thank you, Mistress Constance.' Then he turned and ran. He could smell the rain already; soon big, spattering drops were falling in the dust. Before he reached Mary's Church he was wet through, and the flash and crack of lightning and thunder was like his conscience reproaching him. Barty dived through the porch and sat down against the wall, feeling in the satchel for something to eat. There was most of a venison pasty, a sausage, a lump of cheese. He broke a hunk off the pasty and stuffed it into his mouth.

Constance had even put half a dozen dried apricots into the satchel; Barty nibbled one of them as he stood under the headless statue of Mary and looked out into the High Street. The thunder had gone by, but it was still raining. He waited for ten minutes, and then with a shrug walked out into the drenching rain, back towards Bocardo.

When he stood beneath the dark window and whistled, nobody answered: so he whistled again, louder.

'Lord a' mercy,' a distant voice said, 'whistling in the rain like a stormcock. Who d'ye want?'

'Harry Thorpe.'

'He's asleep.'

'Well, wake him up and tell him to hang the bowl out if he doesn't want to spend the night in there,' Barty said snappishly. He couldn't get any wetter, but there was a cold wind blowing.

There was a muffled exclamation up above, and the debtors' bowl came down, narrowly missing his head. Barty steadied it with one hand, and put in the three coins with the other: and, as an afterthought, a piece of the venison pasty. Then he walked quickly away.

He had meant to go straight back to the college, which after all wasn't far away; but there was a sheltered corner between the chimney of a baker's oven and a garden wall. He draped his gown over the bulge of the chimney to dry, and curled up with his back to the warm brick. Then he dozed off; and woke to find the rain stopped, and the curfew sounding from Christ Church.

Barty scrambled up in a panic, wrapped his gown round himself — it was dry, and smelt slightly toasted where it didn't smell of manure — and pelted back towards the lodge. By luck there was such a rush to be in before the door was locked that nobody guessed he had been out alone. Unnoticed, he climbed the stairs to his usual bed under a library bench.

He had his head down over Aristotle the next morning, surreptitiously finishing the venison pasty, when someone tapped his shoulder. Barty jumped, and looked round.

'Was it you paid my debt?' Harry Thorpe asked.

'How did you know?'

'Guessed.' Harry grinned, and looked at the crumbs. 'Besides, I recognise the pasty. Here.' And he held out a sixpence.

Barty took it up. 'You had it all the time?'

'No, of course not. My purse was hid in my room, but I wasn't about to let them know I was a student, was I? If you'd not bolted I'd have told you where it was . . . only —' Harry sat down astride of the bench — 'only I scarce remembered, when you told me about Giles.' He looked down. 'I tell you honest, Bar, I didn't know. I truly didn't. I was back helping on the home farm all this last two-month.'

'I'm sorry I told you like that, then,' Barty said. He curled his fingers round the sixpence. 'Harry, I must go to Aubrey's — will you come?'

They strolled down the High Street, picking their way across the cobbles, and lingering for a moment to sniff the air outside the Angel, where Jacob ben Simeon was selling the new drink coffee. To Barty's surprise, Constance Aubrey came running towards them before they reached her father's shop. He stopped short, with a sudden ominous sinking in his stomach. 'The book, Mistress Constance — you haven't —'

She said, 'I *am* sorry — I left it in the shop. And my

father sold it.'

Barty almost felt the stones heave under him. Constance was holding out her hand. 'He said I was to give the person who sold it sixpence.' She dropped the coin into his hand. 'I must run back, I shouldn't have left the shop.'

'What *is* all this?' Harry demanded.

'I needed sixpence.'

'What for?'

'Oh, what *do* you think?' Barty snapped, and began to run after Constance Aubrey. 'Mistress Constance,' he said breathlessly, 'who bought the book? Did you see him?'

She looked back. 'Yes, but I don't know his name — a little, thin man with a long nose, and holes in his gown.'

Barty stopped and groaned.

'Whatever is the matter?' Harry asked behind him.

'I sold one of the college's library books, and the Librarian has just bought it back.'

'You're sure it's him?'

'There can't be two people in the University like Short Shenkin.'

'Then isn't your problem solved?' Harry said. 'You take a book from the library, it's back in the library, nobody any the wiser. And you have sixpence. A shilling, with what I paid you back.'

It was very tempting . . . but after a long moment Barty shook his head. 'It wouldn't be right.'

'Proper little Agnes, you are,' said Harry; but kindly. 'Only look, Baa-lamb, if you need help again, come to me. Giles would have wanted it.'

Barty nodded. 'Thanks, Harry. I will.' They turned the corner at the Mitre, and Harry went in to his college. Slowly, with his heart thumping, Barty walked through the gate of his own college, and said to the porter, 'Is Master Jenkins in his room?'

'Shenkin? No, lad, he's in the library.'

Barty gulped, nodded, and went on. It was just as well.

The library was almost deserted. The sunlight slanted

across it, catching a spiral of wood-smoke as it rose through the floorboards from the fireplace in the buttery. In one corner Master Jenkins was slowly turning the pages of a folio volume. Outside, the fiddler was playing again. Barty coughed politely. 'Sir?'

Master Jenkins turned round, blinking. 'Ah — Lambert. You wanted to speak to me?'

Without giving himself time to think, Barty plunged into his story, telling everything except Harry's name. He came abruptly to a halt, held out his hand, and said, 'So I thought I should give you back the shilling.'

'Mm,' Master Jenkins said gently, and stood thinking. Barty's hand began to shake with the strain of being held straight out. 'Aubrey asked a shilling and tuppence for the book, you know,' Master Jenkins said, picking the coins out of Barty's hand.

'I'll pay you when I can,' Barty said miserably.

Master Jenkins turned the coins over and over, seeming to stare at nothing but his fingertips. Then he said abruptly, 'Where are you lodging since Giles Holland died?'

Barty took a deep breath, thought about a lie, and said, 'I usually sleep here.'

'Mm,' Master Jenkins said again. There was a very long silence. Then he said, 'I need someone to sweep my room, carry firewood. There's somewhere in the college you can sleep, I'll find it. Penny a week wages, the first two weeks pay for the rest of this book. Mm?'

It took Barty a moment to work out what was being said; and then he almost choked with disbelief. 'But, *sir* —'

Master Jenkins looked at him. 'No buts. Don't waste your chances. Go and find some food, I don't want my students flapping around like starved crows.' He turned back to the folio: and Barty, after one stock-still incredulous moment, went out of the library and ran whooping down the stairs toward the buttery.

I LOVE YOU, MR. CHICKEN

MARY CAVANAGH

Character: Marjorie, Lady Bullingdon. A thin, frail, elderly lady, dressed in black, and sitting on a Parker Knoll chair. Cultured English accent with the hint of a wobble.

Scene: Elegant sitting room, with lamps lit for a late winter afternoon. Character faces video camcorder.

(Deep sigh.) No doubt some of you will remember me. Those with long memories, I suppose. Old Marje. 10 Downing Street's answer to *'er indoors.* Today I'm honoured to be given this chance to talk up 'my reaction,' and I've certainly got one. This afternoon my illustrious husband, Henry Bullingdon, was buried, and I expect everyone thinks I'm in a state of grievous shock. Ha! Celebration's more the word *I'd* choose. How can I describe the bliss I'm feeling after fifty-two years of sufferance, and who could guess that I tried for most of them to get rid of him? Not by my own hand, of course. Just concentrating like a witch in the hope of creating evil. Oh, the scenarios! Every time the country called for the old sod's head on a plate I longed for suicide, and with every tense, foreign skirmish I would pray for assassination. My favourite was a fatal car crash in a lonely country lane, visualising his severed head flying out of window to land face down on a cowpat. But he actually died quietly in bed. Not here in his own bed, of course. His horse-faced old floozie, Rhona Kent, had the joy of waking up to a corpse, but at least that little hilarity never got out. The newspapers, as you no doubt have

noted, kindly awarded me full respect and honours as the grieving widow. Not before time. I was certainly never awarded any Brownie points as his wife.

Of course I made an heroic effort to present an acceptable image, but it was always an open joke that I never quite cut the mustard. Henry never stopped nagging at me to produce more style and charisma, but I just couldn't choose hats, or walk in high heels, so I always disappointed both him and Joe Public. Socialising presented other dilemmas. My command of small talk was so poor I often found myself stalled in mid-sentence, having completely forgotten what on earth I was supposed to be talking about. Then the rumours started that I drank. In those days I didn't, but being a public Aunt Sally rather led me to the bottle. Mind you, I never gave cause for any real anxiety or showed signs of madness. I was just thought to be a bit fey, and occasionally a teeny-weeny bit sozzled, but I was so insignificant it didn't matter a jot what I was like. As long as I kept my mouth shut, and my breasts covered, my husband's people were happy to ignore me.

(Character leans forward to camera, and lowers her voice.)

No-one ever realised I was just being clever by creating a personal art-form of behaviour to survive the circus. In that way nothing was demanded of me, and I was allowed the luxury of being an invisible *hausfrau* and mother to my children. Not that I fully succeeded. Robert and Rosemary have both had to carry their own battle scars.

(Character picks up a glass of sherry, leans back, and swigs deeply.)

So cheers, m'dears. Goodbye to Henry, Lord Bullingdon of Quantock. Mourned nationwide as good old Bully Boy. The revered patriarchal Prime Minister who resigned after two and a half terms of office without ever being a victim (publicly) of the long knives. The tough war leader, who became an amusing pussycat in retirement, so much in demand on chat shows for keeping both audience and interviewer in stitches. Then, of course, there was his commercial face. The acidic old rogue who sold a million copies of his *Memoirs*, squeezing out all sorts of murky political laundry to soak his colleagues in the mire. He (naturally) emerging squeaky clean and drenched in Lily of the Valley.

Oh, well. There you go. At least I survived the old scoundrel. The only tragedy now is that I'm too bloody old to enjoy my freedom. No salsa dancing or toy-boys for me. All I'll have is the echoing quiet of my own company, the occasional little tipple, and some sweet memories that he knew nothing about. To say I got one over on him is an understatement, but for that little story I must take you back in time, to my youth in the late nineteen forties.

*****

At the age of eighteen it was firmly decided by my powerful mother, and my entourage of aunties, that a career was not for me. I made timid suggestions about training as a nurse, or an infant school teacher, but heads were shaken and lips pursed. Marriage (and motherhood) was specified as my only possible future. These days they'd have got a fruity mouthful and a clean pair of heels, but I was badgered in true Jane Austen fashion to make a good, safe catch. Their criteria (which had changed very little from Miss Austen's list) were that my quarry must be of sound breeding, have excellent prospects, and be good-looking to boot. 'You're a very pretty girl, Marjorie,' they said. 'Don't settle for a donkey.' My father's dogmatic contribution was that my future husband be serious-minded, of high education and, of course, an observing Anglican. Henry Bullingdon suited both agendas with bells and whistles.

Don't ask me where or when we met because I neither remember nor care. Our two families had some sort of cousinly connection, though no-one could quite work out what it was. It was of little consequence. I was the innocent Bishop's daughter who'd hardly been allowed within sight or sound of a young male of the species. He was a gentleman farmer's son, an Oxford Classics don with a vainglorious war in secret intelligence behind him, and ten years my senior. A slow courtship began, and after eighteen months his proposal was delivered in a stammering rush through the window of his Austin Seven, as he was about to drive back to Oxford one frosty night. I accepted because my mother, and the twittering aunties, convinced me that he was the most perfect husband I could ever wish for, and I *had* to be in love. But I was deceived. Conned, cheated, tricked, duped. Blackmailed by other people's enthusiasm, and my own blinkered innocence.

We were married by my father on my twenty-first birthday. A cathedral, fairy-tale affair that spoke of a perfect after-life, but it wasn't long before I discovered I'd married a stranger. A serious intellectual, whom I neither loved, nor even liked very much. Actually, he showed no signs of thinking any differently about me. We moved into a small terraced house off the Woodstock Road, where I gradually found that being an appendage to an Oxford don had its compensations. The slow pace and gentle rhythm of academic life was calm and undemanding. Domestically we settled down, stage-managing polite question-and-answer conversations, and gradually built up a backdrop of small shared experiences. The tempo even became openly affectionate at times, but at night, under the heavy weight of the blankets and the eiderdown, I was forced to suffer the twice-weekly dread of his shuffling over. There was no attempt to talk to me, or caress me, or encourage me to fumble our way into some sort of joint venture. The deed completed mechanically and in silence. Such a silence I could hear the tick of his watch behind my head, and the hiss of the street light through the single sash window. Afterwards a grateful grunt, and pat of thanks on my hip, before turning away to a satiated sleep. It all had to be suffered, you see. In those days marriage was a 'grin and bear it' situation. Young brides set out on the marital path, knowing that their footsteps led to a traditional family life. No twists or turns allowed. No signposts of discontent. Heaven forbid divorce.

After a year the birth of Rosemary genuinely united us with pride, and with the intense needs of a baby I had little time to brood about the shortcomings of my life. With a cheerful sense of duty I washed, ironed, cleaned, cooked, mended, and went to the shops every day . . . Stop, Marjorie! Savour this moment. You must say that short sentence again, slowly. '*I went to the shops every day.*' I went with a mission that superseded the mundane shopping list in my pocket. I went because I'd fallen in love.

Every morning, on the dot of ten-thirty, I directed Rosemary's pram to North Parade; the narrow, double-sided row of hotch-potch Victorian shops, set in the pretty red-bricked heart of North Oxford. Here was provided the housewife's every need, from butcher to baker, greengrocer to ironmonger, chemist to Post Office. As I walked my heart drummed, my armpits ran with sweat, and my eyes were set like a sparrowhawk, desperate for first sight of the painted shop sign:

Arthur Chicken and Son
High Class Grocer
Purveyors of Quality Merchandise
Suppliers of Fine Fare to Oxford University since 1796

I approached, peering through the window for the first shadowy glimpse of the worshipped figure. Putting the brake on the pram and collecting up my shopping bags. My moist palm on the door handle, and the scary, jumping ping of the bell as I pushed. A flush to my cheeks, and a tightness in my chest as I tried to regulate normal breathing.

Mr Chicken stood in command behind the counter; a mature bachelor of impeccable taste and dignity who (in effecting the pose of a *maître'd*) commanded the respect due to his status as a high-class grocer. He was around six feet tall, of solid muscular build, and probably in his late forties. Clean shaven, with a perfectly shaped square head, and his thick, lightly greying hair cut in the usual short-back-and-sides of the times. Always immaculately dressed in a dark jacket, grey pin-stripe trousers, and a red spotted bow tie, this pristine appearance admirably maintained despite his constant contact with cheese, bacon, and loose biscuits. Through the rose-tinted glasses of my desperation, I perceived a likeness to Cary Grant.

There were two assistants in the shop, a softly-spoken elderly man called Mr Glass, and Betty, a busty bleached-blonde who did mornings only. If either of them approached me with a raised eyebrow I turned away and daydreamed with my shopping list. It had to be Mr Chicken. He always smiled when he saw me. A wide, friendly smile of warm recognition and his eyes fixing mine with a special softness. 'Good morning, Madam. I hope that yesterday's cooked ham pleased Mr Bullingdon. I have some excellent brisket today . . . Good morning, Madam. I've had a delivery of the Bath Olivers you so enjoy. So difficult to get hold of in these times, but I hear this wretched rationing will soon be a thing of the past.' His voice was deep and cultured, with no hint of the lazy, stretched Oxfordshire vowels associated with town trade. A voice I'd never known to exist before. A seducing smoothness, long before trained voices on the television compelled the housewife to buy an infinite range of household products she didn't need.

His other unique charm was what would today be called his body language. For a man of such large frame, he was a surprisingly deft mover, swerving around Mr Glass and Betty with the artistry of an ice skater, ignoring their presence completely, and avoiding any physical contact. When standing to serve he appeared to be concentrating intensely, especially when turning the handle of the swishing bacon slicer; holding his head wryly and seeming to ask each dropping rasher if it was worthy of its customer. When weighing dry ingredients he frowned with pursed lips, defying himself to go one minuscule over the requested amount. Then, with swift origami-like manipulation, his large hands folded a square of brown paper to produce a perfect package for the coffee, or the rice or the lentils. This was presented with obvious pride in what he knew to be a deft manoeuvre.

On completion of purchases there came 'the reckoning up'. Having written down the price of each item on a scrap of paper he stood to add up the long column of shillings and pence with his eyelids half closed, and his tongue clamped between his teeth; his calculation completed with awesome speed. After checking once again he nodded with satisfaction and announced the amount with a gentle bow. 'That comes to five shillings and sixpence exactly, Madam. Now please may I have your ration book.'

Being in love with Mr Chicken was exhausting, but I had neither power nor incentive to rid myself of my obsession. It made my real life bearable. At weekends, when Henry was at home, I played an actress's role, being jovial and smiling and happily agreeing with any social suggestions, but I yearned for Monday morning, and the sight of his old black Raleigh disappearing round the corner into Observatory Street.

(Character swigs again at the sherry.)

Things . . . well . . . Hmmmmm . . . Oh, well. Here goes. It was on Monday 25th May 1953, when I began to be invaded by madness. A week when the whole nation felt incredibly loose and happy. The inside and outside of every shop in North Parade was strewn with Union Jacks, bunting and posters of the lovely young Queen, and there was such excitement in the air. The drab, harsh lives we'd led since the end of the war were improving. On the cusp of a new Elizabethan era it was a time to laugh with strangers and step enthusiastically into a bright and better world. I sat at the kitchen table, wrote a shopping list, loaded up Rosemary and set off on the familiar route. I was expecting my courage to fail, but that day I had certainly gulped a huge draft from the bottle labelled '*Drink Me.*'

When I entered the shop I boldly commandeered the attention of Mr Chicken. 'Mr Chicken. Do you still do home deliveries on your half-day afternoon?'

'I do, Mrs Bullingdon. On Thursdays between two and five.'

'Then please may I be included on your round this week? My husband's parents are coming up from Chard on Sunday, and I have a great deal to do.'

'Will you all be watching the Coronation on a television set together?'

'Oh, no. We're even luckier. We have invitations. My father's a bishop and he'll be part of the officiating ceremony. My in-laws will look after my daughter.'

'Lucky indeed,' he said, opening his well-thumbed order book at a clean page and slipping in a piece of carbon paper. 'We lesser mortals will have to be content with the wireless. Now, let me take your address.'

'25 Adelaide Street,' I said. 'The top end. The quiet end.'

He wrote it down with a well-sharpened pencil. 'Now may I have your list?'

As he took it from me our hands briefly touched. His shopkeeper's body movements ceased and he held himself as still as a statue, fixing me with a look that I dared to believe mirrored my own. I stared back, mesmerised, but this fleeting magical moment was instantly ruined. A large woman with two gaberdine-macked children entered the shop, complaining loudly about the weather, Mr Glass called from the other side of the shop, 'Mr Chicken, do we have any more tins of Fray Bentos Corned Beef?' and Betty emerged from the basement steps muttering some complaint about ground rice.

*****

After initial heavy rain it had turned into a hot, steaming afternoon and the doorbell rang promptly at two. He was standing on the pavement, holding a large box containing my order, and I was briefly dumbfounded. My *maître d'* had turned into a grocer, wearing an open-necked check shirt with rolled up sleeves, brown corduroy trousers and a long slub-canvas apron. The unfamiliar sight of his bare muscled arms threw me into a state of such delight my voice came out as hoarse and shaky. 'Do come in, Mr Chicken. I'd be grateful if you could carry my order to the scullery.' He followed me into the house and carefully placed the box where I indicated. Then he hovered, as I thought he might. 'Can I possibly offer you a cup of tea?'

'Tea would be excellent. I've a long afternoon of deliveries due to the festivities.'

I turned the gas up under the simmering kettle and as I waited he came to stand behind me. Nothing was said. I spooned the tea leaves into the pot, poured on the boiling water, and set two Crown Derby cups on their saucers. I stirred the infusion, replaced the lid and stared intently ahead along my line of vision. A dusty cobweb sat behind the gas pipe, a dead ladybird lay on a shelf beside the cruet and the single cold water tap dripped. Through the window an ancient, woody buddleia was covered with butterflies, next door's tabby cat basked in the sun, and Rosemary slept soundly in her pram. Still he said nothing. 'Do you take milk?' I asked without turning round.

'Just a dash,' he replied, 'but please allow me to do the honours.'

In reaching forward to pick up the jug his body touched mine as softly as a shadow. I was aware of his clear, even breathing. I took the jug from his hand, set it down and turned round to look at him. After maintaining eye contact for several seconds he leaned down and kissed me to the side of my eye. As his face touched mine I inhaled the air that surrounded him; a vague mix of clean skin, bacon fat, cheese, Nice biscuits and the sweet briar of pipe tobacco. He lifted my left hand and slipped my thumb inside his mouth, gently sucking each finger in turn until he reached the third. Smoothly, with his teeth, he slipped off my wedding ring, dropped it from his mouth into his palm, and placed it in his trouser pocket. 'What was your maiden name, Mrs Bullingdon?'

'Embury,' I whispered.

'Then allow me to call you Miss Embury.' He then untied his apron, slipped it over his head and dropped it to the floor. This brief moment was my last chance to seek redemption, a split second of delay when I could have rushed from the room in terror; but it was a chance I didn't want.

'Miss Embury. Are you quite sure?'

'Yes. Yes. Quite sure.' And I was. Absolutely sure. I'd spent many lonely hours fantasing this moment with Mr Chicken and what happened in that small kitchen was a version of passion far removed from the narrow parameters of an unfulfilled wife, and a protected bishop's daughter. I rationalised afterwards that no-one teaches birds and bees, and chimpanzees, but with the advent of real desire we're equipped with the primeval lore of the jungle.

It was so, so easy. No reticence, no fear, and no pain. A transporting to a blind dimension where life stops, and the dynamite is detonated, and a hundred tons of stone cleave from the wall-face of the quarry, and two thousand starlings screech out of the cornfield. On the long, quiet descent our lips joined to an intense but gentle kiss.

On release I ran my mouth to his ear. 'I love you, Mr Chicken.'

'I love you, Miss Embury.'

A few moments later he produced my wedding ring, and ran it through his fingers. 22ct gold, but as dull and simple as a tap washer. 'I suppose this had better go back on again?'

'I'm afraid it must.'

'Can I hope that you will become Miss Embury again one day soon?'

I shook my head. 'I'm too busy with the Coronation, and we leave Oxford for good in ten days. My husband has a temporary post as foreign correspondent with the

Daily Courier. He's going to enter politics next year.'

'Ah. So you may live at Number 10 one day?'

'I couldn't bear the thought of it.'

'Then stay. Stay with me.'

'It's impossible. Women like me can't do things like that.'

'You just have.'

I shook my head again, and he slipped my ring back on.

The pot of tea had cooled, but in any case he found he didn't have time for a cup after all. He had twenty orders to deliver. It was getting very hot. The cheese would go oily. The milk would turn. The chocolate bourbons would melt.

*****

Over thirty years later I heard from an Oxford solicitor that I'd been left some effects in the will of a deceased person, a Mr Robert Chicken of the Resthaven Nursing Home in Kidlington. The solicitor, of course, knew who I was. He asked jokingly if Mr Chicken was a secret admirer from my youth, or one of the party faithful. Neither, I said. Just a very nice man I knew from my days in Oxford in the early nineteen-fifties. I was sent a small registered parcel that contained a box and a note of shaky writing. *To Mrs Marjorie Bullingdon (nee Embury). With great admiration and fond memories, from R. Chicken.'* The box held a gold watch, a couple of war medals, and a very old newspaper cutting from a Sunday broadsheet. The headline read:

Henry Bullingdon, the newly appointed Foreign Secretary, pictured yesterday with his wife, Marjorie, and children, Rosemary, 17 and Robert, 15.'

We're all looking straight at the camera, a happy and united family, smiling brightly.

IN PORT MEADOW

GILLIAN RATHBONE

The air shimmered; to be here by the canal must be a bit like being underwater, she thought. The trees on the opposite bank looked no more substantial than their reflections in the canal and sounds were muted as if indeed she were treading on a river bed. Colours merged and mingled, trembled in the heat haze. A sense of unreality made her shiver suddenly and a slight unease caused her to glance over her shoulder.

For heaven's sake — she rebuked herself for this momentary fear — you wanted to get away from people, and yet here you are frightened of being alone . . .

Bathed in sweat she found it difficult to control her bicycle, her hands kept sliding on the rubber grips of the handlebars and the front wheel seemed inevitably to drop into every crack, pulling her up short and making her feel hotter than ever with her growing irritation.

'Oh, it's much too hot,' she moaned. 'If only it would rain, just pour down in sheets right now — at this moment. It'd be so wonderful to get thoroughly drenched and cleansed — I feel so hot and smelly!'

But not far in front the path began to be bordered on either side by high bushes, tall enough to give some shelter from the gruelling sun, and she made for this as someone spotting an oasis in the desert.

However, the bushes were rather dense and didn't afford her the respite she'd hoped for and needed; what's more, they seemed to exacerbate the heat, to close in on her. She began to feel claustrophobic and panicky, stifled; she longed to get out. But there was no way to do so — other than turning back — the canal lay along one side with deep undergrowth leading to a copse on the other. She certainly wasn't going to go by the road now that she'd come this far; she'd stick it out, the bushes wouldn't go on for long. The sweat ran down her neck and back, and from her armpits, soaking her t-shirt. Her damp hair lay in straggly tendrils on her shoulders and the insides of her thighs rubbed together uncomfortably whenever she moved. Even her toes squelched in her sandals.

She wasn't wearing a watch, but guessed it must be about midday; the sun sat scorching high in a cloudless light blue sky. No one was about but, after all, it was mid-week — Tuesday — most people would either be at work, shopping, on holiday, preparing their midday meal, or whatever. So far as she was aware, the only life around resided in a couple of plump ducks (well, you never saw thin ones did you? she told herself, a little hysterically), sleeping seemingly content on the bank, heads snug under brown-speckled feathers. The gaily painted narrowboats she'd passed just now, small net curtains drawn, and plants wilting in their pots on the roofs, had a sleepy look about them too. Either their owners were absent or were drooping inside in the shelter of cool shadowy cabins, because not a sign of movement had come from their direction.

Nothing stirred and yet there was an expectancy about the scene, an imminent explosiveness — or was it something inside herself? Suddenly her insides lurched and, although she was already sweating profusely, a rush of adrenaline increased the flow and her greasy hands nearly relinquished their hold of the bike's handlebars altogether. She'd wanted to be on her own, that's why she was here, pushing her bicycle along the towpath, but she was not alone, not any longer. A slight sound, and from the corner of her eye she saw that someone was there, walking behind her, and pretty closely at that — a matter of only a few feet or so away and making no attempt to get in front of her.

How on earth could she not have noticed him earlier? Where had he sprung from? Had he seen her some distance away and come padding stealthily after her, making a beeline for her — keeping her in his sights until he was well-nigh level with her? And for God's sake, why did he make no move to pass her? He certainly hadn't been there when she paused for a few moments at the lock. She'd propped her bike alongside a notice which forbade dogs without leads and gazed with pleasure on the well-kept little garden of the lock-keeper's sturdy white cottage; she had taken in the scene with its assortment of boats, the paraphernalia of river life, and had fumbled in her bag for a pair of sunglasses. And she had been the sole spectator, or so she'd thought. But had she herself been the focus of someone's attention?

Her heart began to thump so hard it seemed as if it might break through her rib cage and her legs shook so violently she felt it was impossible that he would fail to notice. And she must hide her fear, she must try to act normally. In any case — what a stupid fool she was being, she reprimanded herself. How utterly ridiculous! What was she coming to? Couldn't she take a walk along a common right of way without having terrors about any human being she met en route? Trouble was, of course, his being the only other human being was the reason for the panic . . .

Attempting to quicken her pace imperceptibly, her back rigid with its conscious vulnerability, she pushed her bicycle along relying on it to to steady the uncontrollable wobble in her legs, to take over the support of her body. She let the whole scenario of an attack race through her mind — the grabbing from behind, her being flung to the ground — and then what, the rape or the murder? The violence of her imagination made her catch her breath until she almost sobbed, almost turned to him and said, 'Oh, get on with it, do it, only get it over with!'

How she wished she'd put on a skirt instead of these shorts — they seemed so skimpy now. Was he staring at her, which part of her was he concentrating on? 'Oh God,' she prayed silently, and now tears began to prick her eyelids. 'Oh God, what I am to do? Please take care of me. Please don't let anything happen to me. Please don't let this be the way it's going to be — the end of everything. Please let it be another way — how I'm going to die. Let it be another time, another place, not today; it isn't the right time, the right place.'

All at once, about twenty yards in front, a large dog came trotting into view, its eyes unfocused, dark pink tongue lolling to one side of its jaws, and a narrow collar, minus lead. The lines of hedge were beginning to thin out, and finally end and open up into a field from which the dog had emerged. Not far behind him a young couple were sauntering, laughing and exchanging badinage, hand in hand and oblivious to anything other than themselves and their private world.

Her heart gave a great leap of joy and she felt the skin of her face relax as her set lips curved into a smile. Weak with the enormity of her thankfulness, her body became limp with the gratitude that flooded her being.

Confident in a trice, she glanced round and had barely time to register the scowling face, the stare in the pale eyes, and the cord stretched taut between large red hands, before surrendering to the blackness.

*****

As a self-employed plumber, he'd got a telephone call first thing this morning offering him a big job. Naturally he'd jumped at it; he was up to his eyes in work at the moment, but, working for yourself, you'd got to look at these things in the long-term, to forward plan, as well as dealing with the here and now. You couldn't afford to hang about. The only snag was that his wife was spending a few days at her younger sister's in Didcot — a first baby on the way, due any day now . . . which meant that he'd got the dog to look after while she was gone — and that was some responsibility, particularly with this animal. He couldn't be doing with it at the best of times when he was working, so he'd asked his daughter to take it out with her, look after it for a few hours. And the girl, head in the clouds with another bloke on the go, had said 'Yeah, okay, Dad,' with none of the usual reluctance she showed when asked to do anything. 'Course, she'd have agreed to whatever at the minute . . . She was a mystery to him, well, they all were — women that is — couldn't even fathom out his wife sometimes, after all these years. What made them tick? he wondered, not for the first time.

Anyhow, they'd taken the dog off his hands alright, her and the lad — but without the lead; damn stupid thing to do. I ask you! She knew just as well as he did that the dog was old, had been losing its marbles for some time, and was apt to wander off at the drop of a hat — so he'd had to leave the workplace and come chasing after them with the dog's lead. He'd had a feeling they'd make for this neck of the woods since it wasn't far from home and his daughter had never been overly keen on walking any distance. But that was the modern generation for you, he thought wryly, brought up to go everywhere on wheels. They'd forgotten God'd given them legs.

And yes, just as he'd thought, he was right — there she was — his daughter and the lad who was flavour of the month (how long would *that* last?) — there she was, miles behind the dog which was panting along, almost certainly no destination in its poor befuddled mind, forgetting it was with anyone or going anywhere in particular. But, dippy though it might be, the dog knew a lead when he saw it, and the older he got the less keen he'd become on getting attached to one.

And here *he* was, when he should have been at work earning his family a livelihood, about to try and catch the dog in this baking heat, head beginning to spin from irritation, frustration and the temperature, sweating bricks, his annoyance mounting as the girl pushing her bike just ahead of him made no effort whatsoever to let him get by. Already he'd called out to her a couple of times but without getting any response at all. Like as not, she was in a world of her own, another one like his daughter he wouldn't wonder, brain like cotton wool, dreaming about some man or other.

And then, just as he'd caught sight of the dog and got his lead at the ready in order to pounce on it, the girl had gone and fallen down, passed out practically at his feet. Luckily for her, the bike had tipped over away from her or it could've done her a mischief; as it was, she'd just sort of half-turned and crumpled up.

He'd certainly been glad of the boy's help in lifting her up and setting her to rights — small and skinny as she was, she'd been a dead weight in this heat — and she'd come to in a matter of seconds. But the sun must really have got to her because, as soon as she'd looked up at him, she'd gasped like she was terrified and gone and blacked out all over again.

Well, it was all sorted now — they'd got her and the bike back to his house, and then his daughter's feller had given her a lift home in his van. He'd offered to take her himself, even though he couldn't afford the time. But, as luck would have it, the lad had stepped in and she'd accepted like a shot — unlike her response to *his* offer! Something funny up with *that* one though, that was for sure, drugs or a touch of the sun, who could tell?

Queer thing, the heat, what it can do, addle the brain. What we need, he thought, for the nth time that day, what we need is a nice drop of rain to clear the air, and an end to this dratted heatwave. That'd sort us out, that'd do the trick, one way or another.

A NIGHT ON THE TOWN

ROSIE ORR

Tchaikovsky threw open the glittering doors of the Departure Lounge and strode across the pink marble floor. He was not in a good mood. Paradise was very pleasant, to be sure, but the delightful surroundings tended to have a dampening effect on one's creative powers after a while. Fortunately the Powers That Be had become aware of this (Mozart had gone into a positive decline after a decade or so, and Goya had started picking fights with the archangels after only a few weeks) and these days permitted inmates of an artistic bent to take a trip Outside every year on his or her birthday.

The Excursions Angel looked up with a flurry of wings as Tchaikovsky approached the counter. 'Yo, Pete — blimey, April already? Does time fly, or what? So where's it to be this year, then, Maestro?'

He brushed a speck of fluff from a lavender glove. 'Dear me! It is always so difficult to decide — '

Excursions whipped a brochure from the rack behind him. 'Tell you what. Just been readin' about a little place in wossname — England, yeah, that's it. Oxford, town — no, I tell a lie — city — in the Midlands, dead keen on learning and culture and that.'

Tchaikovsky frowned. 'The English *Midlands*? Really, I hardly think — '

'Seem to go a bundle on your stuff, squire — doin' birthday concerts at no less then three venues tonight.'

The great composer went pink with pride.

'Let's see.' Excursions scratched at an itch beneath his halo. 'Second string quartet at the Holywell Music room — very select crowd they get there, it says 'ere —

plus Favourite Ballet Tunes up the Town Hall. Then there's your Sheldonian, bang in the middle of town and dead upmarket. Gig starts with Romeo and Wossit, ends with the Pathétique —'

Tchaikovsky closed his eyes, weak with pleasure at the mere prospect.

'Take it that's a yes?'

'Da. Oh, definitely *da*!'

'You're on. Now you know the drill. And don't forget this stuff wears off at dawn, so if you're not back by then you'll be tracked as a weather balloon if you're lucky and shot down as a spy plane if you're not.' Laughing loudly, he reached under the counter, produced a small phial and sprinkled the contents over Tchaikovsky's person.

A cloud of silver dust hung in the air for a moment.

*****

When it faded, the great composer had been rendered invisible.

He arrived on the outskirts of Oxford at four in the afternoon, having been so immersed in the problem he was having with the *scherzo* of his new violin concerto (his seventeenth composition in the last month or so; unfortunately, what with the lack of opportunity for sexual intrigue and the absence of money worries afforded by his surroundings, each was more anodyne than the last — dear God, this latest work bored even *him*) that he'd forgotten to alter course at Scandinavia and had carried straight on to Iceland.

No matter: he would be in plenty of time for the concert. He glanced down as he flew, taking pleasure in the unexpectedly verdant terrain with its meadows and canals; momentarily forgetful of his situation he found himself waving excitedly at the oblivious occupants of a gaily decorated barge.

And now here was the city itself! Great Heaven, the dreaming spires looked exactly as they might have in a daguerreotype from his childhood! And look — over there — fellows punting! And surely that was a deer park . . .? He began to lose height, skimming walled college gardens — antique taverns — cobbled alleyways — alighting at last in the middle of a crossroads lined with shops and teeming with pedestrians that bisected the heart of the ancient city. He was about to wander in search of the Sheldonian that Excursions had so highly recommended when he stopped dead.

What in Heaven's name was that extraordinary thrumming sound? That maniacal accompanying drumbeat?

A small crowd had gathered outside a large commercial pharmacy that also purveyed footwear, to judge from its name; many were tapping their feet cheerfully and clicking their fingers. He drew nearer, until he was standing on the edge of the crowd and could see clearly the creators of the disturbance. Five young men — shaven-headed, clad in rags and all seemingly on the verge of starvation — preened and strutted like tone-deaf peacocks as they plucked feverishly at instruments that seemed to be attached to some sort of electrical device.

Ha! They called this cacophony *music* . . .?

Suddenly one of the fellows began to lisp and hiccup and stammer some sort of lyrics — something about a creature called *Pe-heggy Su-hue...*

Tchaikovsky was about to turn away when he found himself analysing the ditty's most diverting syncopated rhythm.

In fact his invisible left foot had begun to tap cheerfully on the off-beat — his shoulders to sway — the fingers of his right hand to click —

*****

The concert at the Sheldonian was delightful — the audience's response most gratifying. As he flew through the night sky on his way back to Paradise, Tchaikovsky found himself humming the *scherzo* of his new concerto. Hmm. It was pleasant enough, to be sure, and yet —

Suddenly he was struck by inspiration.

Of course!! He would add a divertingly syncopated counterpoint for the timpani!!

Oh, how rewarding his trip had been! He would definitely return to this delightful city next year. Perhaps a concert at the Town Hall? Though he must confess the Holywell Music Room had a very pleasing ring to it. . . .

Still humming, he soared over the inky rim of the horizon and on into the darkness, until his voice was lost once more among the stars.

VESTI LA GIUBBA

MARGARET PELLING

That woman's gawping at me. Lady, you didn't really have to stop just there to shift your shopping from one hand to the other, did you? Still, it's not every day you see a Mime parking a bike in Bonn Square on a cloudy Tuesday lunchtime in late March, is it. Make the most of it, I won't be here much longer.

Three weeks in Oxford already. A long time in one place. Oh God, let *her* be here today.

That woman. How long can it take to readjust a bag of shopping? She's got eyes like a frog. And Christ, she's got a birthmark — no, no, it's just a blotchy cheek. But who in God's name would want her? He'd have to be blind. Look at all these others, though, they're just as ugly. The first law of shopping centres: everyone you see is as ugly as sin. *As ugly as —*

Right. Pull your hood a bit further down this time. Then the kids won't see too soon. The kids matter. They aren't ugly.

I keep my parka hood well down, ghostly-monk style, as I unstrap my pedestal from the back of the bike. I tuck the pedestal under my arm and saunter over to the forecourt of the Disney shop. People eye it as I go. What is it about black plastic bin bags that make the things inside them radiate so much mystery?

Now for the transformation. Now to make magic, in this entrance-way to fairyland. Now to show the world that all those years at drama school weren't for nothing. Only almost nothing.

Bloody draughty here today. Oh Christ, I wish I was back in Menton.

Last summer, oh God, last summer . . . the summer to end all summers. But that girl, that bright-haired girl . . . I didn't handle that too well. Dramatics like that could have got me caught. I won't make that mistake again. But I'm not Jean-Pierre le Grand now, I'm Jack Large. The British half of me isn't like the stupid French half, it doesn't make mistakes.

A flick of black bin liner and, hey presto, out comes a white-painted box. Some voice not far behind me says, 'It's him again, Baz.'

No, I'm not. I'm not 'him', not until Baz, whoever he is, can see my costume.

Will she come? She has to, she has to.

There's Dave sitting on his blanket outside the travel agent again. I give him a nod. Depending on how much I make today, I might give him something more. Dave smiles at me crookedly. He'd have a nice smile but for that missing tooth. Don't get your hopes up, mate. Most days you make more than I do, I'll bet.

I take off my rucksack and dump it down beside the box. If the drama teachers could see me now. No dressing room, just this rucksack. No stage, just this white box.

Right. Parka off — like so — and let the white robe tucked up under it cascade down to my ankles — like so. Now the turban. I grab it out of the rucksack and pull it well down over my hair. Any stray hair sticking out? Doesn't feel as if there is. Still, it's a bummer in this line of work, having black hair. One of these days I ought to bleach it. It'd be weird, though. Black eyes and white hair. Ah, what the hell.

Don't get sidetracked, the crowd's gathering. Five so far, stupendous! Off with the trainers, and into the rucksack with them and the parka. Funny how long it took me to work out that wearing socks to these gigs is stupid, they wipe off all the make-up. Still, the thing about socks is they keep the feet warm. I could wear white socks, of course. . . Nah, white socks are for wimps and fashion criminals. Who'd want to be caught wearing white socks.

Don't think of being caught. If you think a thing, it happens.

'He's hardly got anything on. It makes me shiver just to look at him,' one passing woman says to another. Well, ladies, you might just throw me a coin before you go into that nice warm library over there. Not even a fucking five p? Well, sod both of you.

All right, all right, get on with it. The jeans: always the dodgiest bit. For my next trick, ladies and gentlemen, I will with one hand reach under this robe and unzip my jeans, and with the other hand pull them down so quickly that none of you will see what you shouldn't see. And for those of you who wouldn't have minded a glimpse, tough luck.

'He's brave. You wouldn't catch me walking around looking like something from a circus,' says a man in a blue and red striped woolly hat and jeans with patches on them.

'Plenty of people in this town look as though they've escaped from a circus,' says the woman he's with. 'Are you sure it's a "he"? They look totally sexless in that white stuff.'

'It could be a tall "she", I suppose, but look at the shoulders. It's a "he" — it's obvious.'

Thank you, Sir. As for you, Madam, for the avoidance of doubt maybe I'll lift this robe at you. Being arrested in full Mime dress and make-up might be interesting.

Arrested as a flasher. It could add a certain piquancy to life.

Okay, okay, get out the collection box.

I take the box out of the rucksack and put it next to the pedestal. Like me, it's in a game of make-believe. Under the silver paper, nothing but a big biscuit tin, the sort which grannies buy at Christmas with about a hundred different sorts of biscuit inside, including those pink wafery ones which taste of sugared cardboard. Who gave me this pathetic reminder of home, of Christmases at home? Did I ever have a home? Debatable. The agglomeration of bricks and mortar in Highgate containing people I share genes with doesn't qualify, and as for the other one in Cannes. . .

Right. The crowd's got that 'amaze me' look on its collective face. Start the show.

But she's not here yet.

She'll come, she'll come. She must. Now close your eyes and breathe in slowly, and out slowly. Bow your head, arms at your sides. Quite still. Hold it. Now count: one and two and three and . . .

. . . and sixty. A minute, that's it. Now time to make the statue move or they'll get restless.

I raise my head slowly, very, very slowly. One and two and three . . .

. . . and nine and ten. I open my eyes. I'm looking straight ahead. Not bad that time. I'm getting the hang of this moving-but-not-seeming-to-move. Any lawyers or accountants watching? Does this make even types like you believe in magic?

'I wonder who he is,' says a woman in a striped scarf to the man she's with. 'He could be anybody. His own mother wouldn't recognise him.'

Oh yes, she would, Madam. My mother would see through the make-up, she has X-ray eyes. But she wouldn't like what she saw. If she were alive, that is. She's dead now. Very dead.

Those mothers drifting out of the shop with preschool kids stuck to their hands, look at them glancing at me, sighing silently, wondering how soon they can drag little Johnny away. Oh, one or two are actually smiling, like the kids. That's right, forget the rest of the shopping and the chores waiting for you when you get home, be like children again, lost in wonder. Don't be like my mother, spare me ten minutes. Look, I'm stretching out my hands to you, slowly, oh so slowly, but surely.

'Come on Deanne, we'll miss the bus,' says a woman in a pink quilted anorak.

Deanne, inside her red quilted coat, takes her thumb out of her mouth and wails, 'Oh, Mum!' Waste of your breath, kid, Mum's going to win. And yes, there goes Mum, pulling at Deanne's other hand and dragging her off, still wailing. She might have let her daughter throw a two p in the box. Bitch.

I slowly turn my head after Deanne and raise my hand fluidly, gracefully — always my best pose, this — in a gesture of blessing. I let the corners of my mouth turn down. Not hard to do sadness today, not hard at all. Never hard to do sadness.

Where the bloody hell is she —

Oh Christ, she's over there. That's her, coming out of the library with that friend of hers. I only had to wish hard enough to magic her into being.

Don't do a pose for her. Not yet. Just let her come closer.

'He's there again. Hang on, I've got to get him this time,' I hear the friend say — I have bat's ears, suddenly. She pulls a sketchpad out of her bag and begins drawing.

'Sarah, you can't just — you might ask him first.'

'Ask him?' laughs Sarah, sketching furiously. 'Emma, they pose, they don't talk.'

'I thought you'd done all the exam projects by now.'

'Sod the A-level projects, this is real. God, look at the strength in that hand, the way the tendons are fanning out under the skin — go on, *look*. And look at the side of his face. That bone structure, the muscles, the line of the nose, the way the jaw sits — Rodin would've killed to do him.'

'Shh, he'll hear you.' But Emma looks. And quickly looks away again, the way some girls do, the nice ones, the shy ones. Not so many of them around these days. Collectors' items.

Emma. My girl. Would she be, could she be? Would she pass the test? It's a hard test. As other girls have found.

'I thought art that looks like what it's of is so over,' she says to Sarah. 'When we went to Tate Modern you were raving about a glass of water on a shelf.'

'Listen, babe, even the Turner Prize lot would do representational stuff if they were where I'm standing right now — God, that *foot*.'

It's just a foot, Sarah, arranged the way Nature intended. And this hand's just a hand, but I'll give you a better look if you like.

I hold my left hand out, palm upward, toward a boy of about three, beckoning the child closer. The boy looks up at me with big round eyes and takes a tiny step towards me.

That's it, lad, come on, now you're part of my act, it adds interest.

I slowly, slowly, turn my hand over and make as if to pat the boy's head.

Emma's smiling. *Good.* You catch a girl's heart by being nice to kids, not by acting macho.

Come a little closer, Emma. You know you want to.

'Okay, that's it, I've got him,' says Sarah, shutting her sketchpad decisively. The kind of girl who would do everything decisively. The kind of girl who'll go places in this decisive world.

She looks at her watch. 'Hmm, five to two . . . Just time to see if Topshop's got any new stuff in. You coming?'

Don't, Emma. Please.

'I'll just hang on here a minute. I'll see you by the bus stop.'

Oh, yes. Yes.

Sarah throws me a coin. It falls with a clunk in the tin. Two pounds? She can afford it, whatever it is. It's no widow's mite. She gives me an appraising look over her shoulder as she walks away. What am I to her, a man or a subject?

But never mind Sarah. She's not the one who matters.

Right. Gaze into the middle-distance, at that bunch of flâneurs sitting on the wall at the far side of the square. Slowly, slowly. That's it: hold it. One and two and three and four and five and — now, bring your head around toward Emma. Look only at her. She'll know.

Oh, bugger. Oh, *shit.* My nose is starting to run. Don't see the dew-drop, Emma, don't see it! See only my staggering beauty, see me with Sarah's eyes.

That little girl's seen it. Shit, shit! Put your finger down, kid, don't point.

'Mum,' she says. But Mum shushes her, looking embarrassed.

Oh God, what's worse, this tickling sensation or knowing I look like crap. Or knowing there's nothing I can do about it, nothing.

'Right, I'm off,' says one of a pair of secretarial-looking women next to Emma. 'Moira'll be screaming for me.'

'Don't bust a gut, Jane, she's having lunch with that bloke from the Bodleian, isn't she?'

'Susie, she's not having an affair with *him,* for God's sake.'

'He's not *that* bad looking,' says her friend as they drift away.

Other lives, other lives. . . But watching other lives isn't drying up this sodding dew-drop. It's going to fall — now — onto my robe. And now another's taking its place at the tip of my nose. Oh, Christ. And Emma's moving round in front of me, where those two women were.

Right. Damage limitation time. How long have I been here? Twenty minutes maybe. That's it for today. Back to the opening pose: head bowed, arms at sides. *Slowly,* for Christ's sake.

The second dew-drop hits my robe and leaves a damp stain. *Don't go, Emma.* God, I'm shaking, I'm shivering like a leaf, I feel sick. Can a girl do this to me?

The audience shuffles away as I step down from the box. But not her. She's sidled to the other side of the shop doorway, pretending to look in the window at the Mickey Mouse ears sets. But she's actually looking at me, out of the corner of her eye.

Wipe your nose on the robe, quick. . . Now relax. Take it very, very easy. One and two and — turn and smile.

A quick shy smile from her. Blink and I'd have missed it. But it's a start.

Now pick up the collection box and examine the takings. Casually.

Hm. Ten pounds if that. They're cheapskates in Oxford, that's for sure. Still, no dog turd wrapped in a burger paper this time. If I ever see that boy again I'll kill him.

'Sorry, I — I meant to put something in earlier,' she says, coming over and fishing in her bag.

Ah. *Ah.* That's a good girl, Emma.

A five pound note goes into the tin.

'Wow. That's what I call subsidising the arts.' Cue widest smile.

She gives a little giggle.

'My name's Jack, what's yours,' I say, reaching for my jeans. Best not to let on I know her name, that I was listening to her and Sarah. Or that I singled her out days ago.

'Emma,' she says softly, turning to gaze at the Disney displays again as I clamber into my jeans. 'How long have you been doing this?' Sounding a little bolder now. Good!

'Three years. On and off, since I got out of RADA. Makes a change from Shakespeare.' Well, there was that *Coriolanus* in Bradford. I carried a bloody good spear. . . . I grin my best careless Bohemian grin and she gives me such an entrancing smile that my heart turns over.

Heart? Hey, where did that come from? A sudden materialising of something in the cardiac department, and before she's taken the test: not good. Steady, Jack. Steady. But that smile. It's almost enough to take my mind off her hair, her bright, bright hair . . .

'I'm hoping to go to drama school,' she says. 'Not RADA, I shouldn't think, though.'

'Why not?' I say, putting my left foot into its trainer. A stage hopeful. Oh God, what a gift.

'Well . . . you've got to be really, really good.'

'Perhaps you are really, really good. What've you done?' I slip on the other trainer.

'Only school plays. Portia, Nora Helmer, stuff like that. Oh, and Puck when I was in Year Eight.'

'Pathetic,' I say, still grinning. I pull off the turban and shove it in the rucksack. As I smooth down my hair,

I see the pupils of her eyes grow large. Her imagination is whizzing, wondering what I'll look like once the makeup is off. Well, I can arrange for you to find out, dear Emma.

'Look, do you want to talk about this over a drink or something?'

'Oh, er. . . Well, yes. I mean, if you could give me some tips. . .'

I can give you more than tips, Emma of the bright hair. 'Great. Okay, where shall we meet — where do you live?'

'Hill Top Road, the golf course end.'

Hill Top Road. Around the corner from my digs. It can't be this easy, it really can't.

'Ring my doorbell in Southfield Road at eight thirty and we'll decide then which of the Cowley Road pubs it's going to be.'

'All right. I — I'll look forward to it.'

'Until tonight, then,' I say, beginning to shove the white box into its black plastic shroud.

Not a second too soon. Her friend Sarah's in sight, swinging a tote bag. Emma gives me a pink-faced smile and scoots off. Her feet don't seem to be touching the ground.

Right. And now to bid farewell to Dave.

I saunter round to the travel agent's doorway and hand him the five pound note.

'Cheers, mate, have a good one,' he says.

'The Saintly Clown.' I play the part well. Branagh and Rickman and all the others haven't got a thing on me.

*****

As I cycle along the Cowley Road I'm humming.

A quarter to eight. Time to get ready. Best jeans, sexy actor's black shirt. On with the motley, *vesti la giubba*!

On with the motley? Off with it, more like. Bright-haired Emma is going to get the naked face of Jack Large. Whether or not she likes it will determine . . . developments. It could alter the whole course of her life.

Right, the equipment. No point presenting myself for the delectation of Emma if I don't have the equipment to hand.

I rummage in the bedside table drawer under the pile of Kleenex and old envelopes. Yes, here it is. Always ready, in case of need. I take it out and put it in the inside pocket of the jacket hanging on the back of the door, pushing it well down. I don't want it flipping out onto the floor at the wrong moment as it did in Bath. I'm not up to fancy footwork tonight.

So. Lights, action. The scene is set: the wine's open, a little is poured into a glass, and the bed's made in case the impossible happens and she passes the test.

Jack, Jack, don't think of that, don't think at all. Expect her to be like the others, expect her not to pass. Haven't you spent your life expecting the worst and not being disappointed?

Bring down the curtain after the first drink. No need to spin it out and prolong the agony this time, just get rid of her.

Jesus fucking Christ, stop this. Get downstairs and set up the hallway.

I run down two flights. Thank God the old granny who rents me this room is out at her sister's tonight.

I turn off the lights outside the front door and in the hallway and switch on the one in the kitchen, so I'll be in silhouette when I open the door to Emma. Best not to dazzle her too soon with the perfection of my visage. She won't see me properly until I get her upstairs. And then, cue fanfare of trumpets. Taraah!

*****

Twenty-five to nine.

Not here yet. okay, she'll be the sort of girl with just enough sophistication to know you don't turn up on the dot.

Hey, one of the props is missing.

I pull the battered copy of *Love's Labour's Lost* down from the bookshelf, open it at the bookmarked place and put it open side down on the desk. A bit cheesy? It might be, if they ever got as far as noticing the sodding book.

I run my finger along the books. All texts of plays. A bit obvious. I'll add some variety next time. Next time . . . Oh God, can I go through this again?

*****

Twenty to nine.

I pick up the wine glass and take a swig.

*****

Nine.

She's not coming. Shy Emma's thought better of coming to a stranger's digs. Or maybe her mother's thought better for her. Well, that's it then.

Funny. I haven't felt like this before. I thought I knew what disappointment is but I was wrong. Disappointment is what's slapping me in the face right now.

I knock back the glass of wine. Vinegar couldn't taste worse.

The doorbell rings. Some organ under my left ribs does a somersault. When I put my glass down my hand's shaking.

I race down the stairs and fling open the door.

'Hi, sorry I'm late, I had to babysit my little brother till Mum got back,' she says breathlessly. But she's smiling the smile I've had in front of my eyes every minute of every hour since I saw her. Even in the dim light her hair shines, but it's the smile which is blinding me.

'Late? You're early, Emma. Hey, I was just looking at something which might interest you. Come on up.'

'Oh, right. Thanks.'

I keep my face turned away as she comes in and I walk ahead of her up the stairs. 'I've got some wine open,' I say over my shoulder. 'We could drink that instead of going to the pub if you like.' Casual, very casual; let her think it doesn't matter either way.

'Oh, er — lovely.'

Good girl. I don't actually show this face of mine in pubs. And you will very shortly see why.

This thing in my chest, this organ I don't need and don't want, why won't it lie down? I take a breath in, and let it out, slowly. Stage fright. Of all the bloody times to have it.

I open my door and walk in.

Now turn. Slowly, oh so slowly. And smile.

'Welcome to my garret,' I say, spreading my arms wide. And looking her in the eyes.

'Thank you,' she says, with a little half-giggle. She's blushing.

But she's not blinking. And she's not turning away. Christ. But they all blink, they all turn away!

'Let me take your coat.'

I touch her shoulders in helping her out of the coat, but she doesn't shudder. And she sits down straight away on the sofa. What, not a chair, Emma? Won't you hate it if I sit next to you?

'You can tell an actor lives in this room, all those books . . . ' she says. 'Is that one on the desk what you said you were looking at just now? What is it?'

Jesus, she picked up the cue.

'You tell me,' I say, flourishing *Love's Labour's Lost* at her but concealing the title. '"If love make me forsworn, how shall I swear to love? Ah, never faith could hold, if not to beauty vowed! Though to myself forsworn, to thee I'll faithful prove."' Enough. Now look at her full on. Hard. Maybe she hasn't seen. But she must have, she must have!

'Oh . . . I think I've heard it before, but . . . Oh God, you'll think I'm pig-ignorant.'

'I'm not giving you an exam.' But I am, I am. And you seem to be passing it. Jesus bloody Christ. *'Love's Labour's Lost.* Berowne's letter to Rosaline.'

'Oh, right!' she says, her eyes shining. 'The clown mixes up the letters, doesn't he? I saw it at Stratford a couple of years ago, I went with the school.'

'Ah, those school matinées . . . This wine okay? It's a Médoc.'

'Yeah, fine,' she says, looking at her hands for a second.

She doesn't know a Médoc from a mouthwash. Better pour her a big glass, then. And top up my own. I'm in ad-lib territory now, I'm going to need it.

While I'm pouring the wine she picks up *Love's Labour's Lost* and flicks through it. 'I like the ending. "When icicles hang by the wall . . ." England in winter then — you can really feel the cold in the words. Have you been in this play?'

'When I was at school,' I say, sitting down next to her. 'I was the clown.' The one who doesn't get the girl. Can't you see why?

'Can I tell you why I like acting?' she says, leaning a little towards me.

'Emma, that's why you're here.'

'It's because for a couple of hours on that stage you're not you,' she says, speaking so quietly that I have to inch closer to hear. 'You're somebody else. You can be anybody, anybody in the world.'

'Well, cheers to that.' I toast her.

'Cheers,' she says, taking a sip of wine. She looks me in the eyes, blushes again, looks down. And takes another sip of wine. She's nervous. Excited.

This can't be happening to me.

'Are you in Oxford long?' she says, looking at me from under her eyelashes.

'That depends on my agent.' Cue careless laugh.

'Oh of course, right. I suppose all actors have to have agents, don't they.'

'They do. Preferably vicious, snarly ones who can get them top billing and a million grand a show.'

She laughs, and uncrosses and recrosses her legs. Nice legs. Lovely legs.

'What were you last in, Jack?'

'I, er, was playing Stratford, as it happens. Not the main theatre, I was round the corner . . . That was in January and February. Before that — I was in Bath. You have to get used to living out of a suitcase in this business.'

Some truth in all that. But the more the truth, the greater the pretence.

'I wouldn't mind that, I like travelling. Have you ever played abroad?'

'Yeah, last summer. South of France.'

Pretending. Having to talk about it as if it were happening, as if I were on track . . . This is bad. Why didn't she just blink and turn away like all the others. *Why didn't she?*

I hate you, Emma. I hate you.

'Fantastic. Hey, um . . . is there a loo somewhere?'

'Down the stairs, far end of the landing.'

I wait until I hear her footsteps on the stairs. Then I get up and take the cord out of my jacket pocket.

As soon as she comes in. Before she knows anything about it. That's the decent way, she's nice. God, she fancies me. The first one, ever. But I can't take this conversation, it's doing my head in.

I loop the cord around my fingers and twist it. Then I let it go slack.

This is crazy, man. Think about afterwards — you'd have to get her out of this house somehow and dump her in the park. You'd be seen, it's madness. Do it like the others. See her home but don't let her get there.

But I'd have to put up with more talk. I can't, I fucking can't.

Footsteps coming up the stairs. Oh Christ. *Behind the door, now.*

I tighten the cord. The thing under my ribs kicks like a wild horse. The door opens. And in comes a man in costume, a man dressed as a policeman.

'Jean-Pierre le Grand, also known as Jack Large? You are under arrest for the murders of women in Menton, Stratford and Bath.'

*****

'You were clever,' says the Inspector. 'Cup of tea?'

'I wouldn't mind a fag. Preferably not filter tip.'

The man nods at a police officer who looks about

twelve. The boy disappears, presumably to find me a cigarette. 'We've been keeping tabs on you but we didn't have enough to nail you. Which was why DC Shaw volunteered to go and find out a bit more about you. It was handy for her, having to go downstairs to the toilet.'

'The bloke she let in, where was he hiding — behind the garden wall? Hey, is Sarah a cop too?'

'DC Bryden. She and DC Shaw are our new graduate recruits.'

'They were fantastic, they should go on the stage. So, tell me what I got wrong.'

'The woman in Stratford had a trace of white stuff on her coat collar. Forensic analysed it as stage makeup.'

'Bloody hell. And to think that after I've washed I could do a sodding operation, my hands are so clean. Some slap must have got under a nail. Shit. But that wasn't really all, was it.'

'No. There was the, er, artwork on the girl in Menton. As soon as DC Shaw saw you. . . Well, I'm afraid it was obvious.'

'Sure is, without my Dermablend.' Yeah, the Menton girl . . . Still, she deserved it. She didn't only blink, and she didn't only turn away. She said, 'Oh la la, but I thought you would be so beautiful.'

Christ, hurry up with that fag.

At least I didn't carve that portwine stain into the girl's flawless face while she was still alive. It wasn't as if she ever had to see herself in the fucking mirror.

A birthmark. Give it time and it works its way down to your soul.

'By the way, there was my mother, too. Victoria Ramsay, found in woods outside Cannes five years ago, case never solved. I practised on her, you might say. Trust the British police to get me, not the French. You can get away with murder in France. May I have a word with DC Shaw? I'd like to apologise.'

The man smiles, but shakes his head. The twelve-year old reappears with one cigarette. It's a filter-tip.

THE RISING PRICE OF PROPERTY

LAURA KING

'Watch yourselves, I'm heading for the bank again.'

The reeds brushed the occupants of the punt as it crashed through and into a swan's nest.

The incumbent lost no time in expressing her feelings at this assault on her premises.

'Richard! The mother swan's attacking me. Get us out of here, you idiot!' shouted Rachel.

'I can't get the boat to turn. Oh, bloody hell, she's having a go at me now. God, for birds with no teeth, they don't half pack a nasty bite — ow!'

'Well, don't threaten her with the pole for goodness sake, she's only protecting her cygnets.' said Rachel. 'Come back here and let Damien get us out.'

'Make way, make way, let a real gondolier show you how!' Damien strode to the back of the boat while the hapless Richard crawled uncertainly back to his seat.

'Here, have some more wine, Rich,' said Rachel, passing a glass.

Damien raised the pole and plunged it into the water with the exaggerated flourish of a concert pianist. And almost fell in as it refused to be drawn out again and the boat continued moving whilst he remained attached to it.

'You were saying . . .?' taunted Richard.

'It's not my fault, the bloody buggering thing's stuck!'

'Nothing a real gondolier can't handle surely . . .?'

'Only a bit of mud, it'll come out.'

Damien gave the pole a firm twist and yank and it

finally came to the surface — along with the grey-skinned human wrist it had impaled. A larger grey mass below threatened to break water after it. This was too much and the already perilously perched Damien fell into the Isis.

Richard rapidly lost all colour himself, dropped his wine glass and dived for his mobile. Rachel in mid-laugh at Damien's plunge, suddenly realised what was happening, and mirth morphed into horrified scream.

*****

George and Anita Mayhew were the happiest of couples. It had taken a long time to find their dream home in their dream area. Nearly all their lives in fact, and now, after all that dreaming and planning, here they were. Valid members of the Victorian Society at last, with an eccentric pile stuffed from tiled floor to cornice with original features to call their own in the best preserved Victorian suburb in England, replete with a turret for Anita's painting and an oak-panelled study for George. Certainly it required a lot of upkeep, but with seven bedrooms and its central location, it would be easy enough to find a tenant or two willing to trade housekeeping hours for reasonable rent. And a family home should have a family atmosphere . . . .

Anita smiled at the thought of all the young people she might become special to, and who would keep in touch with her and visit years after their time in Oxford, eventually mentioning their wonderful landlady in their memoirs. She might yet enjoy motherhood and grandchildren by default, she mused. And then there were the invitations to foreign climes from overseas academics and students who might board with them. And cats. They must have cats in a home such as this. At least two.

Yes, they would put this house to good use. Every inch of it. Nothing would be wasted and every brick would be lovingly cared for, just as it always should have been. No ghastly PVC conservatories tacked on for them. It would be the homeliest home ever.

But taste being a rare commodity, one of the Mayhews' first tasks was to rip out the aberrant minimalist steel kitchen and install a finely crafted oak reproduction with gothic detailing to echo the style of the rest of the house. A few ill-assorted windows with mismatched glass had also sneaked onto the rear elevation, along with some double-glazed kitchen units. Brilliant white emulsion was covered by Heritage White, stained glass leaded lights were restored around the front door casting a rosy glow over the hallway. Old door furniture was dug out of cupboards and restored to its rightful position.

And the incongruous modern automatic security gates were removed, with reproduction wrought iron gates and railings researched and commissioned.

These they left until last, as the previous owner had been attached to the University experimental psychology department and as such was prone to the odd attack by animal libbers, so the Mayhews made sure their nameplate was prominently displayed on the gatepost and the front door changed from bottle green to Victorian 5 red to indicate new ownership.

The Mayhews soon ingratiated themselves with the neighbourhood, who were by and large delighted to have friendlier neighbours than their predecessors, and so conscientious too. Not only did they attend to all the flaking paint and neglected garden and put up nicer gates, they even made time before church on a Sunday to collect litter on the shared green and strim around the bushes. In addition they kept a good cellar.

And while not of an academic background, they certainly cared passionately about architecture and history.

Only one person had misgivings: Dr Thaddeus Weinstock. He liked the Mayhews and was made as welcome as any other neighbour, but he couldn't get over how Professor and Mrs Jay-Derringer had sold up so quickly, although he knew they had had their house on the market and were intending to take up a residency at the University of Southern California, where it was hoped the warmer climate would improve Mrs Jay-Derringer's rheumatism. In addition, he hadn't received a single e-mail from them. And when he asked the Mayhews for a forwarding address, they replied they were still waiting to receive one themselves, as the J-D's post was starting to pile up and it was becoming a nuisance.

The packers had removed the Jay-Derringers' belongings from the house for storage, but even they had not yet received a forwarding address for its final destination. However, a monthly money order was being cabled from the US to retain it. And when several weeks later Dr Weinstock finally found time from his research into a suspected diabetic gene to contact the University of Southern California, he found that the Jay-Derringers had e-mailed to cancel their residency as one had come up in New Mexico that suited them better.

This struck him as rather odd since he knew of no prestigious university in New Mexico and he spent the rest of the morning surfing the net for one without success. Had they decided to down-shift? He wondered. Professor J-D had talked of getting weary and wanting to semi-retire, if not retire completely, and travel. But no one in their right mind turned down a residency at the USC surely? He thought about trying to contact the J-D's grown up children, one of whom was last heard of in Johannesburg and the other who had emigrated to Australia.

But that was five years previously, when Christmas cards were still being exchanged. Before the huge fall-out over the inheritance, compounded by Fiona's aboriginal intended.

Had the animal rightists got anything to do with their seeming disappearance, he wondered? Surely not. All the activists' forms of attack had hitherto consisted of crude verbs, crude bricks and the odd hoax letter bomb. Whatever they were, they were not international terrorists. They weren't even very good everyday terrorists. And though the Mayhews had by now installed two cats, that did not prove they were animal rights militants capable of harming people they didn't approve of. Besides, they seemed to have no interest in the previous owners, beyond admiring the walnut hall table and grandfather clock they had negotiated as part of the price.

The house in Park Town continued to vibrate with a new life and now two graduate students were often seen mowing the lawn and weeding. A gold-embossed invitation to a Victorian Evening requiring guests to turn up in costume wafted through Dr Weinstock's door and he thoroughly enjoyed every minute of port-sipping, billiards and pontoon in the newly decorated house, while Mrs Mayhew delighted in giving small groups tours of all their handiwork to appreciative 'Oohs, Aahs,' and 'Where did you find it?'

And the Mayhews were so charming and so anxious that everyone should have a good time, he began to wonder how he could ever have doubted them. It now loomed ludicrous in his mind that this genial, vivacious middle-aged couple could be anything other than what appearance suggested.

In fact if he was honest, he liked them better then the Jay-Derringers anyway, who had turned somewhat cranky and ill-tempered since the estrangement from their offspring and the onset of Mrs Jay-Derringer's ill-health, forcing her early retirement from the Taylorian. And they never *had* returned that Loggan reproduction book of Oxford drawings he lent them. Or his mower, which alas, was now packed up and stored along with their other possessions. The Mayhews, however, returned his lawn roller next day with a hand-painted thank you note, no less.

Dr Weinstock made no further effort to trace the Jay-Derringers.

*****

Meanwhile the body in the Isis was making a splash in the local press, suicides and accidental drownings being as exciting as it usually got in Oxford, despite the thriving cottage crime-writing industry. It was eventually identified from dental records as missing estate agent Daniel Crewe-Harrupp — last seen some five months previously, working late at the office. His computer, long since examined for clues, had turned up nothing more enlightening than 'Women in Wetsuits' porn site bookmarks, a few property evaluations and the odd completion document. His personal organiser remained unfound and he had seldom remembered to cross-reference appointments into the office diary. His filing system was equally shambolic, and joyriders had beaten police to his abandoned Audi in Banbury, leaving it a smouldering wreck.

Head injuries consistent with vehicular impact appeared to be the cause of death. Old girlfriends were duly interviewed, and whilst a couple expressed the heartfelt wish that they could claim the credit for Mr Crew-Harrupps' exit, subsequent examinations of their cars revealed nothing, although small quantities of his blood were found around the storm drain cover in the car park of Mercer, Higgins & Wernog. Cruel jokes roamed the internet. Sales of personal alarms went up among estate agents.

*****

Tokyo, San Diego, Lake Geneva, Johannesburg, Cape Town and Barcelona — all in six months. The Jay-Derringers were certainly getting around. The Mayhews were gratified that they seemed to be enjoying their retirement to the full. With the mortgage finally paid up two years previously and the deeds in the Mayhews' possession, they need have no fear that the Jay-Derringers' spending spree would result in any consequences for them, aside from all the special offers that flowed daily through the letterbox.

'Do you know?' said George one day. 'I really think we released them. They were stuck in a rut.'

'Well, they certainly returned the favour,' said Anita.

'For the first time in my life, I feel truly free. This is exactly where I was always meant to be.'

'My dear, we've worked as hard as anybody all our lives. We're only reaping the rewards. And why shouldn't we? We deserve this house. Not least with no pension now to look forward to.'

'Bloody Stansfield-Jonas Pension Society! When I think of the thousands we gave them over the years.'

'Now, don't upset yourself, An. Bricks and mortar are the future now. Everyone says so.'

'But we'll never sell, will we?' said Anita, her eyes darting anxiously.

'Of course not, darling. If we're strapped for cash, we'll just rent out an extra room. Or even turn it into a B&B if we're really hard up.'

'But not flats,' said Anita.

'Definitely not,' he reassured her. 'Now, why don't you show me how that decoupage screen in the master bedroom is coming along?'

'I love gentleman callers in the afternoon,' she purred. 'Particularly in stovepipe hats and drainpipe trousers.'

'And I love 'at home' ladies in silk bustles and well trimmed bonnets,' he teased.

*****

The police continued with their enquiries into Mr Crewe-Harrupp's death. However, the single witness to the car park hit-and-run, a news-blank physics graduate who lodged in a house adjacent to Mercer, Higgins & Wernog had just migrated (minus forwarding address) to a larger room in Headington to better contain his large textbook collection. Not that he was judgemental enough to condemn what others may interpret as 'murder' in any case. Doubtless the killers had their reasons. Who was he to question the decisions of grown men and women?

When the police finally caught up with him (there being sixteen P. Williamses on the University graduate roll that year), he duly denied all knowledge.

Never given to conversation at the best of times, the police soon tired of his monoword, monotone answers, and dismissed him as a standard academic who had his work cut out to recognise himself in the mirror, let alone observe anything useful in the outside world.

The Mayhews were altogether more welcoming.

'Such a dreadful business that. I do hope you get to the bottom of it,' opined Mrs Mayhew as she offered them home-baked teacakes.

'So how many times did you meet Mr Crewe-Harrupp?' asked Inspector Jenner.

'Only the once, I think. When he took our particulars, wasn't it, George?'

'He showed us round the house too,' reminded her husband.

'Of course he did. It was the same day.'

'That's right. We went back after lunch.'

'And then what happened?'

'Well, we decided we were interested,' said George. 'But then we bumped into the owner just as we were coming to the end of the tour, didn't we, An? And he invited us to come back later for a cup of tea. The long and the short of it was that they wanted to move quickly and we wanted to save a bit on fees and things, so they took it off the market and we did it all privately.'

'The estate agents can't have been happy,' said Sergeant Allen.

'We did feel a bit guilty at putting their noses out of joint — if they ever found out, that is. But houses are so expensive these days and I'm sure that kind of thing happens every day.'

'Big commission, though. On a house this size,' the sergeant commented.

'I'm sure they have others,' said George. 'They do specialise in the upper end of the market after all. And doubtless they win some on the gazumping front.'

'Poor man, though. Whatever people say about estate agents they don't deserve to end up in the Isis,' said Anita.

'That's a matter for debate,' replied Sergeant Allen,

betraying his own personal housing crisis.

'Just because you live in one room is no cause for un-professionalism,' berated Inspector Jenner as they drove back to Kidlington HQ.

'Just trying to draw them out,' lied the Sergeant.

'Having a whinge, more like. Draw them out, indeed. I've never seen less likely suspects in my life.'

'That probably means they did it.'

'With home cooking like that and Oxford Civic Society membership? Get a grip, man. Anyway they p***ed him off, not the other way round.'

'I'd almost kill for a house like that.'

'Well, just remember which side you're on, Sergeant. Anyway, you don't have to kill for a house. Just stay with your bloody wife, even if it is only a terrace in Eynsham.'

*****

'Whew,' said George, scooping up a cat and settling back into his favourite wing chair. ' How do you think we did?'

'I think we passed with flying colours,' said Anita. 'Charmed the stripes off them. I never thought I'd hear myself say this, but isn't it great being fifty-five? Isn't it wonderful to be underestimated?'

'I prefer to think of us as just carrying more weight.'

'I don't,' said Anita, patting her expanding girth.

'Okay, then, more gravitas.'

'I love being the people everyone else wishes they were.'

'We've waited long enough to be them.'

'Did you see the envy in the young Sergeant's eyes?'

'Yes, but I rather think you overdid it pressing all those home-made goodies onto them. They practically needed doggy bags.'

'Just trying to detract suspicion, George.'

'And you did. But on the other hand we don't want them popping round every five minutes for a cuppa either.'

'I'm sure they won't.'

'I do hope not. I don't know how long my nerves

could stand that kind of strain. As for anyone poking around in our affairs . . .'

'Why would they, George? Even if they were suspicious, they would need both manpower and competence in order to get anywhere. And how often do you see both of those rare commodities working hand in hand?'

He scratched the cat's chin and she showed her appreciation by joining in with her back paw.

'Good point, my love. Game of monopoly?'

'Oh goody, my favourite!'

Years passed. House prices grew like Leylandii.

Salaries didn't.

The *Daily Mail* continued to claim that the 'average' working wage was £600+ a week — to hoots of derision from its largely 'average' readers, few of whom earned anything like this, and scoured the newspapers and got their eyes tested for all the full-time sits vac they must be missing, paying this — little knowing that the figure was based on a cursory survey of the DM's own staff — just like most of its human interest stories. People who once rented flats now rented rooms. People who once rented a room now shared one. Houses remained empty where no one could afford them (and the rich didn't want to live there), unless converted into bedsits.

The Crewe-Harrupp case was almost as dead as Mr Crewe-Harrupp, except for the odd letter to the *Oxford Times* from Mrs Crewe-Harrupp Senior, to advertise her latest 'Estate Agent Personal Safety' seminar — book now and save £99 — and publicly tongue-lash the police for their lack of results. The police for their part had blown the best part of two years of their budget on 'a bleeding estate agent' and were loath to spend any more on him unless anything came up spontaneously. They did have other crimes to solve after all. Like the young couple discovered posing as the (non-existent) offspring of a drugged and confused 92-year-old for her semi in

Jericho, having foolishly decided to be noisy neighbours, pilfer their victims' bank account and build a new patio in the middle of December. But then it was a first offence.

*****

When the next knock came at the door, the Mayhews were equally ready.

When had they last seen the Jay-Derringers?

'Oh, must be about three-and-a-half years ago now, when we bought the house, wasn't it, dear?'

Anita nodded. 'But we didn't really expect them to keep in touch. We didn't know them or anything. Though I think we got a postcard once.'

'Have you still got it?' asked Inspector Jenner as Sasha the Burmese cat jumped up on his knee and started twirling herself into a comfortable position. Mrs Mayhew smiled at this show of feline over-familiarity with the law. The Inspector briefly made as if to stroke her, but remembering himself, firmly but kindly, lifted off this threat to his authority and placed her on the William Morris rug. She promptly jumped up again.

'I shouldn't think so,' said Anita. 'It would have been a while ago. But I'll have a root around if you like.'

'That would be very helpful, Mrs Mayhew.'

'And I'll put Sasha out. She could do with some fresh air.'

'Thank you.'

'So what's this all about then?' asked George as Anita went through to the study.

'A couple have been arrested using the Jay-Derringers' passports in Thailand.'

'Good God — really? How extraordinary. So where are the Jay-Derringers?'

'That's what we're trying to find out, sir.'

'Mmm. I only wish we could help, but as Anita said, we scarcely knew them.'

'Did they leave a forwarding address?'

'Not for a long time. Then we finally had a telegram with an address in the U.S. on it, so that's where we sent their post for about a year and then we gave up as we felt we'd done our duty if they weren't going to arrange their own redirection.'

'Have you still got the address?'

'Don't think so, but it was care of some professor or other at the University of Southern California. Italian-sounding name. Anita . . . ?'

'Donaldio, Donardio, something like that.' said Anita, coming in from the hall. 'Sorry, I'm afraid I can't find the postcard. But then I don't tend to keep them unless they're from close friends or exceptionally nice. Home-made Madeira cake, Inspector?'

'Thanks. Don't mind if I do.'

'So what have I missed?' said Anita.

'Apparently the Jay-Derringers have had their papers stolen and some couple has been caught using them in Thailand.'

'We suspect it's more serious than that, sir. Since their passports were never reported stolen.'

'How awful!' Anita exclaimed 'They seemed so nice. And they were so looking forward to their travels.'

'Did they tell you anything about their travels?' asked the Inspector.

'Only that they were going to have a bit of an extended holiday before the Professor took up his new residency in California,' said George. 'I seem to recall him saying they'd only ever been abroad for conferences before and Mrs J-D had severe rheumatism. Or was it arthritis? Either way, they obviously thought warmer climes might ease it and give them a change of scenery at the same time. But I don't remember where they said they were going.'

'I don't think they did, George. I think they were just going to do a bit of a tour and decide whether to stay a while in various places when they got there.'

The grandfather clock chimed in the hall and Suko, the student from the Said Business School, was heard to scamper down the stairs and out the front door, shutting it rather too politely for a student.

'I think you're right, Anita. Though it's hard to remember what they said exactly after so long,' said George.

'But that was the general gist of it?' asked the Inspector.

'Yes,' said George. 'I'm only sorry we can't be of more help. Especially if a crime is involved.'

'Well, fraud at least. Thank you for your time. I may need to use up some more of it.'

'Be our guest,' replied George with a smile, and he stood up and shook the Inspector's hand firmly to show he was unrattled.

'Don't look like that,' said Anita as she closed the front door. 'It's not as if we weren't expecting it.'

'All roads lead to the Mayhews, eh?'

'All we have to do is keep our nerve. Oh ye of little faith in Cousin James's talent for paperwork. Not to mention ours for solicitor-nobbling. Thank goodness for corrupt solicitors with a drink problem is all I can say. And we thought they'd died out.'

'Well, they almost did.' He smiled wryly. 'But my point is, what if the police realise that one plus two equals three?'

'Let them. They'd have a job to prove anything.'

'I think we should keep a low profile though. They're getting horribly close.'

'On the contrary, I think it's time you ran as a town councillor and I held a painting exhibition. And what about an Empire evening?'

*****

There were several more police visits, including a search of the house and grounds (volunteered by the Mayhews, before the police could demand it) which turned up nothing, and then impromptu visits by both Josh and Fiona Jay-Derringer, independently of each other, looking for clues as to their parents' whereabouts. They received extravagant sympathy from the Mayhews, who even insisted on putting them up — Fiona and her baby son Galen for what turned into two months, as she wondered whether or not to re-settle in Oxford, following her divorce.

Both offspring blamed themselves for whatever fate had befallen their parents. The Mayhews, plying them with sweet tea and cake, could only let them do so, although Anita felt a slight pang for their torment.

The fuss died away, the children calmed down, the painting exhibition was a resounding success as was the Empire evening with history researched and parts hammed up. George became a popular councillor and all-round friend of North Oxford and its concerns, not to mention running a highly successful campaign to encourage better quality affordable housing in the city and curb the monstrous growth of Brookes University in competition with Oxford University. The police remained clue-poor after the stolen paperwork trail refused to be traced back further than twenty-one months and two changes of hands and all the Mayhews' information checked out. And then salvation. A fringe group calling itself 'Animal Avengers' stepped in claiming responsibility for the Jay-Derringers' disappearance, 'as a warning to other vivisectors'. No evidence ever materialised to substantiate this claim, but it still came as a welcome respite for the police, who at last found someone to arrest and thus a result to announce after months of red herrings and dead ends.

*****

Some years later a book came out by Professor P. Williams entitled 'My Life in Physics'. Luckily no one read it or they would have found a lengthy account of how, as a graduate student, he had watched from his room as, next door, a middle-aged couple slugged an estate agent to the ground and then mowed him down in his own car, in his own car park, finally bundling him into his own boot, while he had been struggling with a reversible and irreversible processes essay. And this, for some reason, was the catalyst for P. Williams realising a whole new theory of energy conversion, eventually leading to his illumination as an illumini.

As for Anita, she was busy reading glowing reports of herself in the autobiographies of her 'boys and girls' that were beginning to emerge from down the years, gratified that she had given them such a taste of 'genuine Oxford', such an 'oasis of refuge amid a mad, consuming-frenzied age' as one of her 'boys' had put it. Another had even set up a scholarship as a result of his 'happy times' there. And of course all left the Mayhews' auspices with a whole new appreciation of architecture and what constituted good taste.

Some say it was the shock that killed them, when first George, and then Anita, died within days of each other, he at the breakfast table and she sitting on the sofa as she watched the evening news.

To other viewers, the news that a 30-year-old executive Langdon development in Wolvercote was suffering severe concrete fatigue due to construction using sub-standard materials, and the subsequent evacuation of a young family from one house, would probably have seemed everyday news. But for the Mayhews it was the end. They'd known modern houses were abysmal, even temporal in quality, but this was ridiculous.

And then to confirm their worst fears, bones were found protruding from one of the foundation cracks of the said house. And the Mayhews had no need to wait for laboratory tests to rule out animal origin.

Even concrete overcoats, it seemed, weren't what they used to be.

But they'd done their bit for art, architecture and life, and the house would live on.

Until their next incarnation . . . .

WYTHAM WOODS
AT TWILIGHT

SHEILA COSTELLO

I'd never seen the woods in that half-light. Mysterious, full of shadows. I always left well before dark. But that afternoon I slipped up. I came out of my hiding-place in the hollow of a tree and saw the sun close to disappearing on the horizon.

I'd got carried away. When things were bad at home, I slunk off to the wood and sheltered in the tree where no-one could find me. I played around, scratching words on the bark inside with a stone. No, not Jason loves Madeleine. I knew quite well he didn't love me any more. I scratched words like rabbit, badger, deer and sometimes I scratched pictures of them too in flight through the bushes. You can say I'd gone funny if you like. Maybe I had. But it gave me a break from Jason and his superior smile, and the arguments, and the feeling that things were falling apart.

It was the bison that held me up that afternoon. I was getting above myself by then and I'd started on a picture of a bison. The glow from a candle lit up the tree hollow. I felt like some old cavewoman sitting in her den scratching out images of favourite beasts. Outside the air had grown chilly and an early firework sent sparks across the moon. Late October. The nights drew in quickly now. I stepped out of the hiding-place and realised time was against me. I had to get back to the car. Soon it would be pitch-black.

I knew Wytham Woods like the back of my hand. I'd spent half my childhood there, walking to and fro from my grandmother's house in Eynsham. But in the dusk, with mist beginning to rise from the ground, I took the wrong turning. I ended up on a track I didn't seem to remember, in a clearing where the trees loomed like ghosts all round. Something grey and sleek broke cover and darted across my foot and in the distance a larger animal crashed through the undergrowth, heading in my direction.

I had the strange idea that the bison had sprung to life and was coming after me. I shot off along a side path to get away. A squirrel winked at me out of a hole, its small eyes glittering. Rooks flew up like bits of charred paper. The damp leaves squealed as I trampled them down. Everything in the wood was closing in.

Then the noise started, a kind of hissing. And it might have been the wind shushing in the trees or the steamy sound of a giant breathing. Or the bison might be drawing nearer. Or a wolf. He'd never got me as I walked to my grandmother's house all those years ago but he could still have been lying in wait.

In a panic I ran wildly through the trees. I must get to the gate or be trapped all night in the shadowy wood with whatever monsters lurked there. Jason went out early on Saturdays. He went to the pub with Kevin from work and Mike from the bowls team. He wouldn't know I wasn't home. And by the time he came back with a few drinks inside him, he wouldn't care. It might have been the ideal solution to his problems anyway. I tore through brambles, over streams and across ditches until, sobbing with relief, I came to the main path. A shower of rockets went up and for a minute lit the way. Friendly fire.

The gate was shut when I reached it. I had to crawl under the fence. My jacket had been ripped to shreds by the brambles, now it was covered with dirt and dust. But I was out of the wood. The car was parked in Wytham. Not far to go.

With the hissing sound still in my ears, I raced on towards the village. The lights of the first house I came to were ablaze. The place looked welcoming and warm. I relaxed and a few minutes later rounded the corner into the lane where the car was parked. Then I froze.

Slumped against a wall near the pub was a figure in ragged clothes, his body bent forward. He wasn't moving but the wind flapped the rim of his battered hat. My heart thudded so loudly I could hear it. Was he dead, was he alive? Was he sitting there ready to pounce on anyone who walked past? Any second now the arms might shoot up and the face might turn to look at me. I didn't know if I had the strength left to run again. I'd done enough running for one day.

I clamped my hand across my mouth and the figure slowly swivelled round. I'd expected a full-grown man, instead a sturdy, filthy boy of around nine stared straight at me. He waved. And after he waved, he grinned.

'Trick or treat, miss?' he said.

WORD GAMES

MARY CAVANAGH

May 1954

I had a Gran once, but she went off her head. She was my Mammy's Mammy, and she lived in James Street. We used to go to Gran's on Tuesdays. Mammy always said, 'We're going to be very busy today, darlin', and I don't think that old school will miss you. We'll go up and see Gran and get a sub.'

A sub wasn't a submarine. It was something out of Gran's purse. Gran would open her purse, and rummage around, and complain, but she always found a little sub. 'You'll be the death of me, Annie,' she'd shout, snapping her bag shut.

When we got home the nuns always came knocking on the door looking for me. 'Brendan's been ill today,' said Mammy. 'Terrible pains in his tummy.'

'You're a little liar, Annie O'Dowd,' said Sister Mary Martha. 'You'll rot in hell, you wicked girl.'

'I'll thank you to call me Mrs O'Dowd,' said Mammy.

'Oh, and I'm Princess Margaret,' sneered Sister Evangelica.

Gran was fat with long, grey greasy hair. She smelled like cheese. I knew Gran didn't like me, but once, when she'd been drinking out of a bottle called Rich Ruby, she started talking funny and pulled me onto her knee to kiss me. My throat started going woomp, woomp, woomp, and when I struggled to get off her she shouted at me, 'The buckles on those bleeding sandals of yours have ripped me to shreds, you little sod.' My sandals weren't bleeding. They were just a bit scuffed and dusty.

Every time we went to Gran's there was a row about something. Gran was always telling Mammy she was a dirty slut, but Mammy wasn't. She used to spend an age in front of the mirror with her creams, and paints, and scents. She always looked in the mirror and said to me, 'Well, Brendan. Don't you think your Mammy looks just the ticket?' A ticket was something the bus conductor gave you. Mammy didn't look at bit like a ticket. She looked like a film star.

Gran called Mammy a scrubber once, and they had a fight. A real fight. They were always fighting like boys do. But Mammy was a scrubber. That was true. She went to the Convent of Notre Dame on the Woodstock Road every day and she would get some hot soapy water, and a tin bucket, and a brush. She tied some cloths around her knees and spent all morning scrubbing the floors. At the end of the week the nuns gave her some money, and sometimes she got a bag of clothes for me. 'Old cows,' said Mammy. 'They can stuff their hand-me-downs up their tight arses.' I didn't think the nuns looked like cows. I thought they looked like magpies.

On the day we went to Gran's for the last time everyone was talking about a man called Roger Bannister, who had broken the four-minute mile. We walked up in the freezing cold to look at a big field, and Gran put her hands together like she was saying her prayers and said, 'This is where it actually happened. Can you believe it? Mr Bannister broke the four minute mile right here on our own doorstep.' I couldn't understand why Gran was so pleased and excited. If I broke anything she shouted at me, and smacked me.

When we got back to Gran's Mammy sat down at the kitchen table. The kitchen was cold and smelled of gas and stinky dishcloths. She was moaning about the cold misty weather ruining her face and she got out her make-up bag. She started dabbing her cheeks with her powder puff, but Gran came up behind her, and shoved her shoulder, and called her a vain little tart. Mammy's mirror flew out of her hand, crashed down on the quarry tiles, and smashed into a million pieces 'That's seven years bad luck you've given me now, you old bitch,' yelled Mammy.

'You make your own bad luck, Annie,' said Gran, pointing her smelly finger at me. 'That little bastard, for instance. Pity you don't know the difference between a lucky black cat and a randy Tom, and even more of a pity you couldn't finish his face off properly. Hares only cross the path of the wicked.'

Mammy jumped up and screamed so loudly my ears hurt. 'I'll kill you,' she yelled. 'I swear to God I'll kill you. How dare you belittle him? He's a beautiful child. Isn't his life going to be tough enough without you rubbing salt in the bloody wound?'

Mammy then picked up a saucepan. She made a big lunge at Gran and tried to hit her so Gran ran up the stairs. Mammy ran after her. They started struggling with each other on the landing, snapping and snarling at each other like two dogs in the street, but I wasn't afraid. It had happened so many times before, I thought it was quite exciting. But then Mammy put her foot behind Gran's ankle, and pushed her hard, and Gran toppled over and came tumbling down the stairs, bomp, bomp, bomp.

'Oh, holy shit,' screamed Mammy, and she flew down the stairs, two at a time, but at the bottom she had to jump over Gran. She grabbed her bags and pushed me out of the door into the little front garden. She slammed the door so hard the windows wobbled, and then she turned round and yelled through the letter box, 'You're an evil old witch, so you are.'

Mr. Bradshaw next door was sweeping his path. I liked Mr Bradshaw. He always said hallo to me and sometimes he gave me a toffee. He just stood there, with his mouth hanging wide open. Miss Primandproper on the other side was polishing her door knocker. She never used to speak to Mammy and me, but she looked round sharply at all the commotion. 'And what the bloody hell are you two gawping at?' Mammy shouted at them.

'Fishwife,' hissed Miss Primandproper. Mr. Bradshaw blew his cheeks out.

Mammy shoved me out of the front garden into the street so hard I fell over on the pavement and scraped my knee. 'Oh for God's sake Brendan, get up,' she yelled, and marched off down the road talking to herself. She went so fast I had to run to keep up with her.

'What's the matter with Gran, Mammy?' I asked her.

'She's off her head, Brendan,' she said. 'She's completely and utterly off her head, and that's the God's honest truth.'

That puzzled me. I thought she looked completely off her legs.

When we got on the bus I asked her, 'Mammy, what does "belittle" mean?'

Mammy smiled sweetly, and ran her finger down my cheek. 'Oh, she thinks you be too little, so we'd better get cracking and feed you up so full you'll go off bang, but it won't be tonight. We didn't get a little sub and I've only got two bob, so it'll have to be fishcakes.'

Mammy fried the fishcakes and hotted up a tin of spaghetti. It was my favourite dinner of all. She washed my face, lit the fire, emptied all the ash trays, puffed her scent around the room, and changed her frock. Then Mammy got out my colouring book and crayons. 'Would you like to do some colouring in, Brendan?' she asked me.

'I'd rather you read to me from my book, Mammy?' I replied.

I had a book. The nuns gave it to me, and it was called *The Wind in the Willows*. Mammy started to read, but she had to follow the words with her finger, and she was very slow. I didn't mind though. I just loved to hear the words,

'. . . *The Rat, much excited, kept close to his heels as the Mole, with something of the air of a sleep-walker, crossed a dry ditch, scrambled through a hedge, and nosed his way over a field, open and trackless and bare, in the faint starlight. Suddenly without warning he dived; but the Rat was on the alert and promptly followed him down the tunnel to which his unerring nose had faithfully led him. It was close and airless, and the earthy smell was strong . . .'*

'Oh, darlin',' Mammy sighed. 'Mole's house sounds a bit like this old basement. A damp dump in the bowels of the earth. How I wish we could close our eyes and be whisked away to somewhere lovely and bright and sunny.'

'Toad Hall!' I said, sitting bolt upright on her knee. 'One day we might live at Toad Hall.'

'Do you know what I'd like, lovely?' she replied. 'I'd like a great big house in the country with a huge garden where you could go out to play, and you could run and run and run, until you were so puffed out you couldn't run any more, and when you stopped to get your breath you still wouldn't be able to see the end of the garden. Fat chance of that happening because your Mammy's a fool.'

Mammy started to sniff and sigh and dab her eyes. 'Brendan,' she said. 'Your Daddy could have been so many things. A Texas millionaire, or an English Lord, or an Indian Prince. Why did he have to be a fish porter from the Covered Market?'

I couldn't understand it either. My father didn't go to America and make a lot of money, he failed to become a member of the Royal family, and he didn't change the colour of his skin and wear a turban, so why did he hump fish when he had so many other choices? 'Miss Primandproper called you a fishwife today,' I said. 'Perhaps she knew my Daddy.'

Mammy laughed and cuddled me. 'You're so funny. That dried up old maid's never known anyone like your daddy, and that's a fact.'

But then there was a hard knock on the door and Mammy threw up her hand to her mouth. 'Brendan,' she said. 'You love Mammy, don't you?' I nodded. 'Then you won't let Mammy down, will you?' I shook my head.

There was a big man at the door wearing a belted raincoat with a trilby hat. On each side of him stood two big policemen with serious faces, and their tongues poking through their lips. 'Miss O'Dowd,' said the man in the mac. 'I'm Chief Inspector Branigan. I have some very grave news. I'm sorry to have to inform you that your mother has been found dead. It seems she fell down the stairs.'

Mammy just went all mad. Screaming, and moaning, and holding her head, and rushing about and touching things. 'Oh, Holy Mary, Mother of God,' she wailed. She whirled about and fell on her knees. 'Oh Mammy, Mammy,' she cried. 'Please forgive me.'

She looked up at Inspector Branigan and made her loveliest face. 'We had a little quarrel this morning Inspector,' she whispered, 'but it was just our way. We never meant no harm. All a storm in a tea cup. Now I'll never be able to say sorry.'

'Yes, I know,' he said. 'Her neighbours, Mr. Bradshaw and Miss Lamb, said there'd been a bit of bother. Perhaps we can have a chat about this little quarrel.'

One of the policemen took me into the kitchen and he told me some jokes.

'Doctor, Doctor, I feel like a pair of curtains,' said the man.

'Well, pull yourself together,' said the doctor.

'Doctor, Doctor, I feel like a window,' said the man.

'That must be a pane,' said the doctor.

We started playing 'I-Spy' but then Inspector Branigan came into the kitchen and lifted me up onto the table. 'How old are you, Brendan?' he said.

'Five,' I said.

'It's sad about your Gran, isn't it?' he said. I nodded. 'You saw her this morning, didn't you, Brendan?' I nodded again. 'You and your Mammy were probably the last people to see her alive. Brendan, do you know what happens to people who don't tell the truth?'

'They rot in hell.'

'That's right, son. And what happens to them if they're even too wicked to go to hell?'

'I don't know.'

'The nuns eat them. I don't want you to rot in hell, Brendan, and I don't want the nuns to eat you. I want you to grow up to be a big boy, so if you tell the truth you won't rot in hell, or get eaten up, will you? Now, Brendan. What was your Gran doing the last time you saw her?'

Mammy had come to stand in the doorway. Her face was white and tear stained, but her eyes were bright blue. Her head was shaking and wobbling on her neck, and she was twisting her hanky in her hands. 'Well, Brendan,' said the Inspector. 'Tell me the truth. What was your Gran doing the last time you saw her?'

Mammy was looking so frightened I wanted to say what she wanted me to say, but I didn't know what that was. I looked at her, but she just looked back at me with bright blue sad eyes. I didn't want either of us to rot in hell, or be eaten by the nuns, so I knew I had to tell the God's honest truth.

'She was completely and utterly off her head,' I said.

WALKING PACE

MARGARET PELLING

Oh. It wasn't there. She must have flipped it off when she tied her jacket sleeves around her waist. 'I've dropped something. It can't be far, I'll go back and look for it.'

'Dropped something?' said James. 'What do you mean, dropped something?'

Oh, this nit-picking precision of his. Why couldn't she just drop something? And why couldn't the weir over there be a way of making water sparkle in the sunlight, not 'part of the river management scheme', why couldn't the big round holes in the path be doorways to burrows, not 'hazards to walkers which should be filled in'?

'All right, it's a pedometer,' she said.

'A *pedometer*?'

'Okay, okay, I just wanted to check my fitness, that's all.'

'I've just spent the last hour on the Thames Path with a woman who's secretly wearing a pedometer. Well, well.'

This was the man she was going to marry in a fortnight. It said so in her diary.

'Look, go on, will you?' she said. 'It must be back there towards the trees, it won't take me long to find it.'

'And if it's fallen into the long grass?'

'Well, I'll be unlucky, won't I.' She turned and started walking, fast.

'Sue, we've got to be back in Oxford by five,' came his voice after her. 'You can't have forgotten about Mum?'

Forgotten about Mum? If only she could. These Sunday teas at his mother's, was she marrying them too? The hints that maybe she shouldn't go for the head-of-year promotion at school because they'd be having babies soon, was she marrying all that?

'If I don't catch you up by the time you get back to Clifton Hampden, leave without me,' she called over her shoulder. 'I'll get a train from Culham.'

'But there aren't any trains on a Sunday!'

'I'll hitch a lift, then!'

'Sue, for God's sake, what's got into you today?'

She didn't answer.

The pedometer had only cost a few pounds but she'd have paid more than that for a few minutes of peace, alone with bushes blazing with hips and haws and other berries she couldn't name but it didn't matter, and the fat, squat spire of Appleford Church across the river. She fingered the diamond on her left hand. Why on earth did she put this on today? Stupid to wear jewellery on a country walk. She took it off and put it in her pocket. When she flexed her third finger, how light and free it suddenly felt.

There was that pretty green narrowboat again, still moored by the bank, the one with the Labrador sunning itself on the roof between the pots of flowers. Was there anybody on board? It didn't look like it. The dog lifted its head as she passed and gave her a doggy smile.

Oh God, it was just nerves, wasn't it? It had to be, all the arrangements were made, even the bridesmaids' dresses were finished. James was a good man, he was never selfish or moody, and he loved her. She was bloody lucky, just think what the ones before him had been like. So what if he didn't always sparkle.

She turned and looked back the way she'd come. James wasn't in sight, but he couldn't be far away. If she ran back now, she'd catch him up.

Ah. Was that the pedometer?

She bent down. No, it was only a beer bottle top.

As she straightened up, the dog on the narrowboat started barking. 'Hello!' came a shout.

So there was someone on the boat, a man. She turned, but before she knew what was happening, she'd overbalanced and landed flat on the ground, her foot caught in a rabbit hole.

'Sorry, I must have startled you,' called the man. 'Are you all right?'

She tried to get up, and winced as the pain seared through her foot.

'I don't know,' she called.

'Don't move.' The man jumped for the bank.

When he ran his fingers over her foot, his touch was gentle, but at the same time firm. He seemed to know what he was doing. So when she said, 'Ow, that's where it hurts,' it was no surprise when he replied, with a smile, 'I thought it would be. Trust me, I'm a chiropractor.' Nothing was broken, which was a relief, but she'd given the ankle quite a sprain and walking was going to be dodgy for a few days. The least he could do was give her a lift home.

At a guess, he was thirty-something. Her own age, or perhaps a bit older: there were faint smile lines etched in around the eyes. The eyes themselves were the nice brown sort, she couldn't help noticing. You could sit and talk to eyes like that and lose all track of the time.

'A chiropractor who lives on a boat?' she said, as he pulled her to her feet.

'Chiropractors have to live somewhere. But I see patients on dry land, I share a practice in Abingdon with some other alternative types. We've got a herbalist, a homeopath — you know, the usual suspects.'

'It's okay, I've been to an aromatherapist. Once.'

He laughed as he swung her onto the boat. He lifted her as effortlessly if she'd been the smallest child in her class, not their nine-stone teacher. As he settled her into a folding chair in the stern, the dog jumped down and began licking her hand.

'Back off, Nelson, you haven't been introduced,' he said. 'I'm Craig, by the way.'

'Hi Craig, hi Nelson, I'm Sue.'

'I hope you're not in a hurry,' said Craig, 'this boat goes at walking pace.'

Walking pace? They'd take hours to get to Oxford. Well, as the only alternative was swimming there, she might as well lean back and enjoy the ride.

'I'm not in a hurry,' she said.

As he was unmooring the boat, she caught sight of it. The pedometer. In a patch of thistles.

ABOUT THE AUTHORS

Jane Gordon Cumming's story was written for a competition run by the Oxford University Department of Continuing Education, and it was subsequently broadcast on BBC Oxford. She has also written stories for magazines such as *Woman's Own* and *Bella*, and had short humorous pieces on Radio 4. Her first novel, *A Proper Family Christmas*, was published by Transita in 2005, and her second, *Changing Course*, is due out from Transita in 2006.

Lorna Pearson lives in Oxford, mainly in the Bodleian Library. She has written nine novels and numerous plays, filmscripts and stories, besides academic articles for the 'The Dickensian' and 'The Conradian'. Her one-act play, 'It', was performed at the Burton-Taylor Theatre, Oxford, in 2005. As L Pearson she is the author of *Mad Dust Country*, 'a fable for every American century', available from Amazon.com.

Angela Cecil-Reid spends her days teaching in Oxford and shepherding her rare breed sheep. Written in her elusive spare time, her short story 'Arthur's Boy' was commended in the Sid Chaplin Short Story Competition while the opening chapters of her current novel for children, *The Dream Cat*, reached the regional shortlist in Waterstone's Wow Factor Competition.

Linora Lawrence works for the University of Oxford, has had articles published in Oxfordshire's Limited Edition over the past ten years, is now writing short stories and is working on a novel. She believes it is impossible to live in a city that has produced *Alice in Wonderland*, the *Narnia Chronicles* and Philip Pullman's *His Dark Materials* without absorbing some of its special magic.

Gina Claye is a writer and storyteller. Her children's poems have been published in anthologies by Scholastic and Oxford University Press. Her collection of poems, *Don't Let them Tell You How to Grieve*, is used by Cruse Bereavement Care to help those who are grieving.

Chris Blount has enjoyed writing throughout his life, making time as a family man and during his career as an investment manager to participate in writers' groups. He had hoped to invest more energy in this hobby after early retirement, but running his own business has certainly foiled that dream.

Jane Stemp published two novels for teenagers, *Waterbound* and *Secret Songs*, both with Hodder, in such spare time as she had while working as a librarian for the University of Oxford. She is now a rare books librarian for the Royal Navy, with an 80-mile weekly commute which leaves her wondering where she finds the energy.

Mary Cavanagh teacher-trained in the 1980's and her English course spurred her into creative writing. 'I Love You Mr. Chicken' was joint winner of BBC Oxford's short story competition in 2004, and was subsequently broadcast. With 'Word Games' she was the winner of the Oxford Times/OUDCE short story competition in 1999. Her first novel, *The Crowded Bed*, will be published by Transita in December 2006.

Gillian Rathbone's literary output includes lexicography (the Oxford English Dictionary), the compiling of a dictionary for learners (Macmillan's), history and nature articles (the *Oxford Times* magazine 'Limited Edition'), the winning of several short-story competitions, and *Bus Stop Poems* published in 2004, with her general collection of poetry soon to follow.

Margaret Pelling took half a lifetime to remember that her first love was making up stories. Along the way there was research astrophysics, then the Civil Service, and then one day 'Yes, Minister,' became 'Goodbye, Minister.' '*Vesti la Giubba*' reached the regional shortlist for the Real Writers Award 2003. Her first novel, *Work for Four Hands* (Starborn Books), came out in summer 2005.

Rosie Orr lives in Oxford. Since winning the South Bank Poetry she has had poems published in several magazines and anthologies. She is currently working on a novel.

Laura King describes herself as 'A celebrity trapped in a nobody . . . a thirtysomething office worker by day and popular stand-up performance poet by night, who writes the odd short story and aspires to break into radio.' Her sparky comic poetry CD 'Whoops, wrong planet!' is available from LauraKingsey@hotmail.com

Sheila Costello has had two children's novels published by Oxford University Press: *The Cats'-Eye Lighters* (1991) and *The Box that Joanne Found* (1995). Both were published under the name Anne Lake. She used to work for a local bookseller and has been interested in writing since junior school when she won the class prize of a bar of chocolate for the best story every week for a year. This is the only prize she has ever won!

The authors would like to thank Chas Jones for all his help and advice and special thanks to Radmila May for her painstaking and diplomatic editing.

Printed in the United Kingdom
by Lightning Source UK Ltd.
112390UKS00001B/94-255